ONE BONE
ANTHOLOGY 1

ONE BONE
ANTHOLOGY 1

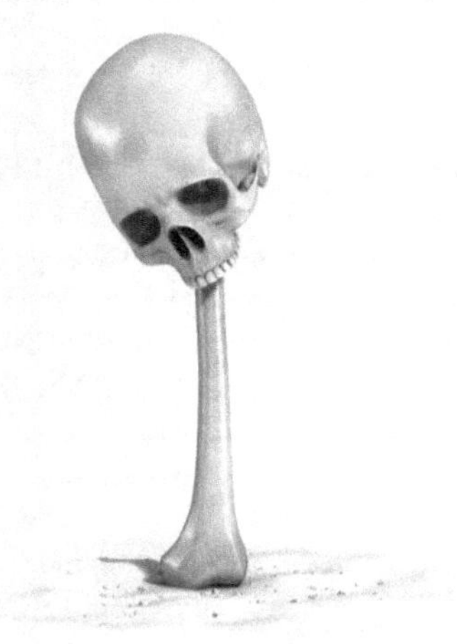

T.K. WRATHBONE

☠ Royal Star Publishing ☠

Skull & Bone is an imprint of Royal Star Publishing
www.royalstarpublishing.com.au

Trade Paperback ISBN: 978-1-925683-80-6
Large Print Paperback ISBN: 978-1-922307-00-2
Case Laminate Hardcover ISBN: 978-1-922307-01-9
Dust Jacket Hardcover ISBN: 978-1-922307-02-6
Next Top Mannequin e-book ISBN: 978-1-925683-17-2
Cinderfella and Princess Charming e-book ISBN: 978-1-925683-19-6
www.BadLuck-YoureDead.com e-book ISBN: 978-1-925683-21-9
The Bones Of Wrath: Changes e-book ISBN: 978-1-925683-23-3
A catalogue record for this book is available from the National Library
of Australia.

Cover design: Royal Star Publishing and Odyssey Books
Cover photos: istock.com/koya79
Typesetting in Minion Pro by Royal Star Publishing

CONTENTS

NEXT TOP MANNEQUIN

CHAPTER ONE

"Come on, Macy, we'll be late." I excitedly dragged my best friend along the path to the front door of *The Top Modelistè Fashion and Beauty Agency*.

"All right, all right, stop pulling." Macy pulled her arm from my grasp and stepped up to the sign above the door. "I can't believe we signed away our holidays for this," she groaned, but the huge grin on her face gave away her true thoughts.

I knew she was as excited as I was that we'd scored two free places in the summer modelling course we were about to start. While modelling wasn't really our thing, we knew all our fave celebs had gone through this school at one stage or another. Most of the contestants on *Next Top Beauty Queen*, Shelle Overdrive, our favourite lead singer of our favourite band *The Mechanics* had done a course, and even Toni Deltucci, the host of our favourite TV show *Mind Your Step*, one of America's hottest music shows, was a graduate.

And now, thanks to seeing the advert in the local paper for a chance for two to win a two week modelling and etiquette course, we had won the competition and would be graduates ourselves.

I came back to reality when a small group of girls stopped behind us. "Are you going in or what?" one asked.

My head spun around to see who was talking, and I offered a quick apology. Macy and I pushed open the doors and rushed into the lobby. We all came to a halt at the reception desk.

"Are you girls here for the new two week modelling course?" a blonde lady whose name tag read Samantha asked as she stood to greet us.

"Yes," we all replied in unison and giggled.

An older blonde woman walked through a door on our right, and we watched in bewildered excitement when we realised it was Patrice Pellcott, owner of Top Modelistè, and mentor and teacher to all who came through her doors.

I felt my eyes widen so as to take in every detail.

"Girls," Patrice called with a swift clap of her hands. "Welcome to *Top Modelistè*, and welcome to your two week modelling and etiquette course. We will be doing a lot of fun things this week, and hopefully, I will make graceful models out of all of you. If you'll please follow me, we can get started."

Macy and I exchanged wide-eyed looks, grabbed each other's hands, and with hysterical butterflies in my stomach, we followed Patrice through the door she'd come through.

It opened into a long red and very glossy hallway with huge frames featuring pictures of graduates on both walls. Mannequins stood beside each frame wearing the same outfit the graduate was wearing in the photo.

"They look so real," Macy whispered in my ear.

"Their eyes are following us," a girl behind us said. We turned and looked at her long blonde hair and pale blue sweater set. She gave us a slight shrug. "Well, it's true," she whispered.

Patrice stopped at the last photo and mannequin. "And this is Melanie Matuk. She graduated from *Top Modelistè* twenty-five years ago. She was our first graduate and a top role model for all the girls who came after her."

I stared at the photo, studying Melanie's features and outfit, and then looked at the mannequin. It was wearing the same fairy floss pink print dress that Melanie had on in the photo. I stepped closer and stared into the dummy's face. It had the same nose, mouth, and eyes as Melanie's. I glanced to the photo and back again. The eyes were exactly the same colour as Melanie's and they were…moving…

What!?

I gasped and jumped back.

"See," the blonde girl from before whispered in my ear. "Their eyes follow you. It's creepy. You saw that, right?"

I gulped and glanced from the girl to the dummy. The eyes didn't move now. I gulped again as Patrice spoke to us.

"Is everything all right, girls? We need to move on now."

I looked around at the group of girls I was with and saw them all looking at us. Macy nudged me and I caught her look of freaked out urgency.

I saw Patrice's scowl and jumped a third time. "Everything's fine."

Her scowl disappeared. "Good. Let's move into the work station." She spun on her heel and strode through a door on our left. "This is where we'll be for the first week."

I saw tables and chairs lined up across the room, while around the outside against the walls were individual dressing tables with huge lighted mirrors. They were the kind with the big light bulbs you see in movies.

"Take a seat at a table and I'll run through what we'll be doing."

I pulled out the closest chair and sat down behind a table while Macy took the one beside me. I felt a little weird. I couldn't describe it, even if I tried, but it was more than butterflies doing cartwheels in my stomach. And I was cold, even though the doors were closed and there were no windows. I pulled my light coat around me and shivered a little.

"All right, girls," Patrice called and clapped her hands. The other girls calmed down and sat quietly while I waited with bated breath. Patrice slowly paced back and forth. "You will be here at *Top Modelistè* for two weeks. That includes working this weekend."

A groan went around the room.

Patrice put her hands up. "Enough of that. You

all signed up for this course except for our two winners, so you knew it was going to be for twelve days with a graduation two days later. Now..." She stopped at her desk and glanced at something. "The two winners of the win a Two Week Summer Course Competition are Macy Compton and Dell Chester." She looked up. "Will you girls please stand."

Macy and I glanced at each other and stood.

"Ah, there you are. Welcome and congratulations on winning our yearly free spots in a *Top Modelistè* summer school course. Which one's which?"

"I-I'm Dell," I stuttered, nervous now the butterflies had returned. I studied the other girls in the room. All were perfect looking blue-eyed blondes. Some looked a little older, some a little younger, all looked annoyed that we had won a free pass to the course. It was a course that usually only rich people could afford to send their rich daughters to.

"And I'm Macy."

I turned to watch Macy. She didn't seem nervous at all. "Dell and I are twelve, and we love *Top Modelistè* and *Next Top Beauty Queen* and all the shows that *Top Modelistè* graduates are on."

"That's nice, dear," Patrice replied coolly.

"And we've been *totally* looking forward to this course since we first found out you were giving two places away in the comp. We applied *hundreds* of times," Macy went on. "*And I've never been so excited—*"

"All right, girls," Patrice cut her off. "You can sit down now and I'll continue."

I partly tuned out her monologue as I eyed off our rivals. I felt a little weird again, as if I was in some bad movie. In fact, I felt I had seen these girls before in some bad movie. All blonde and blue-eyed. I noticed that when they'd all stared at Macy and me when we were standing. It reminded me of a movie I'd seen, but had not been *technically* allowed to watch. I'd stood in the doorway to the lounge while my parents watched late night TV. It was a movie about a small town where all the women were having babies at the same time, and those babies grew up fast. *And* they all looked the same. Blonde and blue-eyed. I shivered again. Not only had that movie scared the wits out of me, but I had nightmares for weeks, and now it seemed like I was in the middle of it.

I glanced at Macy who seemed hypnotised by Patrice. We were the only dark-haired girls in the course. I studied Patrice as she went on about week two. Middle aged or older, gold hair pulled into a bun, a sharply cut soft blue skirt suit with a white ruffled blouse. Patrice Pellcott had been a high fashion model back in her teens and twenties. After a string of successful businesses she'd set up *Top Modelistè* twenty-five years ago and hadn't looked back.

"And once the course is over we will end with graduation on Sunday evening when you will be presented with your certificates and sashes, followed by a three course meal with your families." She clapped her hands again. "Okay, girls, today's lesson will be about skin, and the best cleansing routine for you. Dell, please come and hand out the fact sheets and we'll get on with the lesson."

I all but jumped out of my chair at the mention of my name, and meekly rose before moving to the front of the room. I quickly gathered and handed out the papers to everyone then sat back down.

While Patrice started telling us about skin types and what they meant, another girl handed out small trays with tiny bottles, cotton wool and buds and a little flat plastic thing that looked like a knife. I lifted it up to look at it.

"That's a spatula," Macy whispered.

I looked at her quizzically then picked up the small blue bottle that looked like the one Patrice was holding, and that's when the fun commenced.

For the next three hours we used beauty products called cleansers, toners and moisturisers, using the spatula and cotton wool to paste our faces in sweet smelling smooth as silk creams that made my face feel tingly and oh so soft.

When our four hours were up, we bade Patrice goodbye and ran outside to find Macy's mum waiting to pick us up.

"How was it, girls?" she asked, driving off into traffic.

"Good," we replied in unison and giggled.

"Bet you can't wait till you get back tomorrow?" She smiled at our enthusiasm.

I didn't reply, but listened to Macy as she gave her mum the rundown on what had happened. I shivered again and thought about the mannequins and how I could swear their eyes had moved.

"All right, we're home." We pulled into the Comptons' driveway and Macy and I got out. "What will you do for the rest of the afternoon?" she asked.

"Can we go to the park?" Macy asked. "We'll ride our bikes."

I had left mine there as I'd ridden to Macy's that morning so her mum could drive us.

"Sure, but be home no later than five-thirty. Your brother's got soccer practice."

"I won't forget," Macy called as we gathered our bikes and went cruising ten houses down the street to a small park that was smack bang in the middle of our road.

Yep, Macy and I lived in the same street, her at one end and me at the other, so we were always at the park in the middle and our parents knew where to find us.

We rolled over the hilly terrain, dumped our bikes beside the swings and jumped on. Pumping our legs, we tried to see who could go the highest, and Macy won before we slowed down to a slight rocking motion.

"What did you think of today?" Macy dangled her legs and kicked at little tufts of grass in the dirt below her.

"It was good." I was leaning back looking up at the fluffy white clouds above us.

"*Only good?* I thought it was awesome. The whole place looked just like it does on TV. Pictures and posters of all their graduates everywhere. And those make-up dressing table mirrors with all the light bulbs are so awesome. I want one. I wonder if Daddy could make one for me."

"Mmm," I mumbled, thinking about all the pictures and the mannequins.

"Didn't you enjoy yourself?"

I glanced at her and saw her intense gaze. I blinked in surprise. "Um, yeah."

"But?"

I searched among the playground for the right words. "Um, it was a bit creepy, you know, that hallway with the mannequins. They look so real and lifelike."

"Of course they are. They would be," Macy cut in. "They're made to look just like each graduate."

"That's just it." I turned my swing around so I was facing her. She did the same. "They not only looked *exactly* like the people in the photo, it's like they *were* the people in the photo. Those dummies were so lifelike I could swear their eyes moved."

Macy shook her head in amusement. "Dell, this should be right up your alley. You love ghosts and ghouls and creepy things. You'll probably make up a really good story about it for English class when we get back next year. I can just see it now." She threw her hands up in front of her and spread them out to make headlines. "'*The Ghosts and Ghouls of Top Modelistè*', or, '*Meet the Dummies of Next Top Mannequin, by day they stand in the hallway at the office of Top Modelistè, by night, they strut the catwalks of fashion week'.*" She collapsed into fits of laughter. "Oh, Dell," she gasped. "You're awesome. You know I love your stories, but there's no story here." She glanced at her watch and grabbed her bike. "I'll see you tomorrow."

"Okay," I called and watched her ride away. "I hope you're right, Macy. I hope you're right."

CHAPTER TWO

Tuesday morning, Macy and I raced into the building of *Top Modelistè* and saw the other girls already heading for the workstation. Quickly following, I raced down the middle of the hall of mannequins, and kept my gaze firmly planted on the ground so I didn't have to look any of them in the eye. Taking our seats, we saw trays of make-up in front of us, and picking up a tube of lipstick, I saw 'Bubblegum' written on the bottom.

"Okay, girls," Patrice called out as she came marching into the room and up to the front. "Today is all about make-up. Yesterday we learned how to take care of our skin on the outside, and today we talk about what goes on for special occasions. If you look at the container featuring all the little coloured squares, that's called eyeshadow." She picked one up from the tray in front of the girl in the first row. "Some of you may already know what all of this is, but some may not. Eyeshadow goes on your eyelid." She picked up a tube and some coloured pencils. "This tube is full of mascara. You put it on your lashes, and these pencil-like things are called eyeliners. You line your eyes with them. They are not to be confused with these," she added as she picked up some more pencils, "which are lip liners. You line your lips and then apply lipstick." She put the other things down and picked up several lipsticks. "Like this, so that the colour does not bleed onto your skin. There is also powder, blush, foundation, and a variety of concealers." She put everything down. "Please move to one of the dressing tables against the walls and we'll begin." We carried our trays over to a table and sat down, ready to start. "First you will clean your face with a wet wipe make-up remover and then I'll show you how to begin."

We took a wet wipe each from the small packets on our trays and then Patrice picked the girl from the front row to use as a guinea pig. "Please watch carefully how I do this. We will do it one side at a time."

We all watched as Patrice carefully spread what's called serum over the girl's face. I struggled to remember her name, but realised I didn't know any of them.

Turning to our mirrors, we copied what Patrice had done. I noticed it had no smell, was white, and it completely disappeared once I rubbed it in. After that, we applied foundation, cover-up and powder.

"Now with blusher, you take your pot and your short fat brush. This one," she said and held up a black-haired blush brush. "Swirl it around in the pot, tap it on the side, and then lightly stroke it along your cheek bone from beside your nose to beside your ear." I watched intently as Patrice repeated it for the other side of the girl's face.

Picking up my brush, I swirled it around the blush pot, tapped it on the side, and then brushed it along my cheekbone. I leaned in close to the mirror for a look.

"Pretty good," Macy piped up beside me.

I turned and looked to see how she'd done, but it was more like overdone. I giggled and she screwed up her face.

"Guess I should have swirled lighter." She grabbed a tissue and frantically wiped at the dark pink smear on her face.

"Remember, girls, swirl lightly," Patrice reminded everyone, and I saw she was looking in Macy's direction.

I finished off the other side and put the blush back on the tray.

"Next we have eyeshadow." Patrice picked up the rainbow palette along with a long stick with a little brush at the end of it. "You dip the brush in gently and sweep it along your eyelid like so. Now, for a bit of fun, I want you to try every colour in the palette and make note of the ones that suit you better. Does it suit your eye colour, your hair colour, and your skin tone? Have fun, and don't forget to wipe off each colour before you put a new one on." She stopped and stared at the door. "I'll be back in a few minutes girls, have fun." She quickly left and shut the door behind her.

The room erupted into excited chatter as we all went crazy with the eyeshadow, applying every colour to our eyelids and making new colours in the process. Macy and I looked at each other and laughed. She'd brushed it past her eyelids and into her hairline.

Patrice returned. "Okay, girls, wipe off your eyes and I'll come around and help you pick the right colours for you."

We quickly tissued off our eyes and within a minute or two Patrice was beside me tilting my head back and forth while her finger was on my chin. "Brown hair, green eyes, cool complexion." She looked down at the palette. "This peach for your upper eye, this green for the lid and this liner." She handed me a teal eyeliner before moving on to Macy. We finished off the day by learning how to apply mascara and having our photos taken.

"Tomorrow we will talk about health on the inside." Patrice collected the trays. "You can learn how to keep yourself healthy on the inside with good food and water. See you tomorrow, girls."

I hung back while the others raced out of the room because I wasn't looking forward to going back down the hallway.

"Ready, Dell?" I heard Macy say and came out of my daydreaming.

"Um, sure," I muttered, and we quickly left. I averted my eyes to the floor and saw Macy's feet disappear ahead of me.

"Hurry, Dell, Mum's waiting." Her footsteps

faded and all was quiet.

"Help."

I stopped. My heart pounded in my chest and I finally looked up.

"Help me."

I was terrified. I flew around in circles looking for the person who could have spoken, but there was no one there. I didn't even hear Patrice in the work room and the receptionist wasn't in the lobby.

"Help me."

I panicked and spun around looking from the pictures to the doors to the mannequins. My eyes stopped on the one closest to me. It was supposed to be Sara Tomorrow, the graduate from last year, but she looked slightly different. The eyes. The eyes looked different. The eyes looked big. The eyes looked bigger than they should be. The eyes looked real.

"Dell?"

I jumped ten feet in the air. "Um, yes?"

Patrice came over to me from my right. "Is everything all right?" She was cool and collected in her powder blue skirt suit and ruffled blouse.

"Um..." I bit my lip, hoping she wouldn't see how shaky I was. "I was just, um, taking a closer look at the pictures and mannequins." I glanced at Sara Tomorrow. "They're um, so lifelike."

"Yes." Her eyes narrowed and she peered closely at me. "That's the way they're meant to be." Her right forefinger tapped her left hand as they lay clasped in front of her.

"Dell, where are you?" Macy called out. "We have to go."

With the weird little spell broken, I regained my composure, and after a quick goodbye to Patrice, who was watching me ever so closely, I sped down the hall, out the door, and just beat Macy to her mum's car.

"What was that?" she asked as we climbed in. "Did Patrice call you back for something 'cause you looked scared out of your brain."

I realised I was panting. From racing or fear? I wasn't sure, but I looked at her and shrugged. "Just talking. Can we go to the park when we get home, Mrs Compton?"

"Of course, Dell, but as usual, be home by five-thirty."

When we got to Macy's we grabbed our bikes and pedalled to the park. After dumping mine, I threw myself on a small green mound of grass.

"Okay, out with it!"

I looked up to see Macy in front of me, hands on hips. "Out with what?" I wrapped my light coat around me even though it was a warm day.

"What were you *really* doing in that hallway?" She sat down beside me. "You looked like Casper the Ghost when I saw you."

I took a deep breath and told her how I'd heard someone calling for help, and then Patrice telling me how the dummies are meant to look lifelike. "She's actually kinda scary," I ended with.

"Dell!" Macy exclaimed. "Do you really think a

mannequin called for help? This isn't one of your stories, you know." She shrugged. "They're just made out of plastic or something. They can't talk." She brushed a strand of hair behind her ear. "Not that we know of."

I glanced fearfully at her. "And it's that part that I'm worried about, Mace. The part we don't know about."

CHAPTER THREE

I don't scare easily. In fact, I rarely scare at all. I can watch all kinds of disaster end of the world movies or shows, vampire, zombie, you name it, I *rarely* scare. But this was different. This was a weird even I couldn't explain. You know how with a portrait of a person, sometimes it feels as though their eyes are following you around the room? Well, it was *that* kind of weird. Times by one hundred, no, a thousand. Creepy weird. Creepy come to life weird, and it was only the third day of the modelling course.

We quickly hurried down mannequin hall and into the work room. Today was all about eating healthily and I found this kind of boring. I kept sneaking glances behind me to the door that led to the hall, thinking a mannequin would be standing there peering at me with her very real eyes. I tried to concentrate, but just couldn't, and when the class finished I tugged on Macy's arm.

"Don't run off this time," I whispered. "Let's walk slowly and have a good look, then you can tell me if they look real or not."

Macy sighed and rolled her eyes. "Really, Dell? Haven't you gotten past this yet?"

We walked out the door and carefully looked at each mannequin until I stopped halfway. I stared, knowing something was wrong. I looked from the picture to the dummy.

"Boo!"

"Argh."

Macy laughed, bending over to slap her knee. "Gotchya!"

"Not funny, Macy," I scolded, watching her straighten up. "Look at this one. What's different about it?"

We peered closely, our eyes flitting back and forth. Macy sighed in my ear.

"I've got it," I whispered excitedly. "The mannequin's in a different position."

"What?" Macy leaned back. "What are you talking about?"

I looked around at the others, making sure they were in the exact position as the graduate was in the photo. But this one wasn't. "Look." I pointed. "All the others are standing the same, but this one is standing in a different position to the person in the photo. It's moved."

Macy frowned. "Dell! Are you telling me you think the mannequin changed positions itself? Patrice probably moved it, or one of the girls bumped into it. Come on, you've really taken your imagination to the extreme this time." Rolling her eyes, she walked off down the hall.

I went to follow, but a small movement caught my eye. I turned back and looked. The arms hadn't moved; nor had the head. But when I looked at the face, those very real looking eyes now looked glossy.

Not the actual glossy kind of glossy, but the tears welling up about to cry kind of glossy. And as I stood there watching, a very real looking tear slowly rolled out of the eye socket and down its face.

"Mah, mah, Macy." I tore down the hallway, out the door, and to her mum's car.

"What took you so long?" She straightened her seat belt.

I slammed the door, locked it, jammed my belt into its holster, and looked up at Mrs Compton's stunned face. "Floor it, Mrs C!"

She gave me an arched brow. "*Floor it, Dell?* Do I get an apology for slamming my door?"

"But I…" I glanced from her to Macy's shocked expression and back again. "Sorry, Mrs C. I just wanna get out of here." I looked out the window and saw Patrice staring down at me from a top floor window. "Please, can we go now?"

After arriving at the Comptons', we raced upstairs to Macy's bedroom where I threw myself under the quilt on her bed.

"Oh, for goodness' sake, Dell." She yanked back the quilt. "What's wrong? What happened to you?" She sat down beside me. "You came flying out of there like a ghost was after you. I thought you were right behind me, but I got to the car and Mum asked where you were." She grabbed a bed cushion and bopped me on the head with it. "So what happened? Did one of the mannequins come to life and chase you like a ghost. Wooooo…" She waved her fingers in front of my face. "Wooooo…"

I sat up in disgust and crossed my arms while she kept doing it. "No, it didn't come to life and chase me. It started crying."

Crickets…

I turned my head and raised my brows waiting for her reply.

"It what?" Her hands dropped beside her.

"Mmmph," I mumbled. "Gotchya there. It started crying. A tear rolled down its face. I'm telling you, Mace, something *weird* is definitely going on in that place. Those mannequins are *way* too real." I got up and paced the room. "I felt it. Felt it from the day we started that something was weird and not right." I stopped and chewed on my bottom lip while I thought about it. "The place *has* to be haunted, Mace. *It just has to be.*"

"Delany Jane Chester," she scolded from the bed. "There is *no such thing* as ghosts. The school is not haunted, and it's just your imagination at work. The mannequins *are not* real and one *did not* start crying today—"

"But you didn't—"

"Stop it, Dell." She stood up so she was face to face with me. "You're being silly. Why are you so afraid of mannequins? Did one fall on you as a baby?"

I scowled at her amusement. "No."

"Well, then." She picked up a bunch of model magazines. "What's your problem then? Here." She shoved some at me. "Get your mind off it and read the latest Modelistè Mag. It's got a great story on Shannon Ryder from *Top Ten Two*."

I grabbed the mag and sat down to read about one of our fave bands, but couldn't take my mind off what had happened.

*****

Thursday morning I didn't even want to get out of bed, let alone out of Mrs C's car outside the school. I didn't want to walk inside the doors, let alone down that red glossy hallway, but I found myself surprised when Macy called out that they were gone.

"Gone?!"

"Yes, Dell, they're gone."

We stood in the doorway and looked down a long empty hall. Well, not quite empty as the pictures and posters were still hanging there, but there were no mannequins…

…At all!

I heaved a huge sigh of relief and felt a huge weight lift from my shoulders. We hurried into the work room just as Patrice walked in with a bunch of coloured material.

"Good morning, girls." She laid the bundles on the table in front of her and continued, "One of you asked earlier where the mannequins were. Well, they had to go in for maintenance. It seems one of them got water on it and had to be dried out."

I heard an intake of breath beside me and glanced at Macy. She gave me one of her 'I told you so' looks, but I ignored it and turned away.

"It also seems some of the others have some damage and need to be fixed."

A few of the girls glanced back at me and I frowned. What were they looking at me for? And what were those smirks about?

They turned back to Patrice.

"We're going to talk about colour today and find out which colours and shades best suit you and what tone you are."

"What's a tone, Patrice?" one of the girls asked.

It's funny. Here we were on day four and I hadn't even met or spoken to the other girls. I still didn't even know their names.

"Let me explain it to you while I show you." She pointed at me. "Dell, I'll start with you. Please come up here and sit."

Recovering from my surprise at being chosen first, I wandered up to the front of the room and sat on the chair facing everyone.

"First of all, I'll cover your hair." She wrapped a white towel around my head, turban style, covering my hair. "We need it to block out the colour of your hair so we can get an accurate reading of your skin tone. Next, we'll cover your clothes as well." She wrapped another white towel around my neck so it completely covered my clothes. "Now, what I'm going to do is hold up a piece of gold metallic material under Dell's face, and I want you all to tell me what you see."

I looked down at the shiny gold fabric.

"Head up, Dell."

I obeyed the command as one girl called out. "She looks sick."

"Yeah," another piped up. "She's all yellow."

"Exactly," Patrice said. "The gold represents the warm tone, and when it clashes with its opposite, it will make you look sick. Which means Dell is not a warm tone." She whipped the gold material away and replaced it with a silver one. "But a cool. See the difference? She doesn't look sick anymore. It's because she's a cool tone and silver is her base metal."

"Cool," I said. "I like silver jewellery."

"Then you already intuitively knew what you were. Now we'll do your colours." She held up four different swatches of material one after the other, asking questions as she went. Turns out my favourite colours are my best colours and I'm a 'summer'. In simple terms, there are four seasons of colours, summer, autumn, winter and spring. Summer colours are bright cheerful shades, while autumn are muted tones, winters are dark, and springs are nice bright pastels, although there are also many variants in these seasons and different shades to suit different people. Patrice handed me a metal ring with rectangles of coloured plastic.

"These are your colours, Dell. Carry this set with you so you can match up your clothing colours in store. You can pick the right shade every time and look great without spending extra money. Who's next? Macy?"

She removed the towels from me and Macy and I exchanged places. Being a dark redhead with green eyes meant Macy was a warm tone and her season was autumn. Most of the other girls were spring or summer being blue-eyed blondes and all.

We learned about the colour wheel and how two colours can make a third. Colours opposite each other on the wheel are complementary colours, and those beside each other are analogous. We all tried to pronounce it, but fell into a fit of giggles.

"An-al-a-gus," Patrice said once more.

"An-al-a-gus," we repeated after her.

She also taught us different combinations of colour and how they all blend and worked together. "All right, girls. You have your colour wheels; they're yours to keep. Don't forget your colour packs, and tomorrow we're going to learn about types of fabric and how to mix and match patterns and styles. See you tomorrow."

"Bye, Patrice," several of us muttered as we walked out the door. The mannequins weren't there and I felt much happier than I had in days.

CHAPTER FOUR

Friday morning the mannequins weren't back and I was still happy. We stumbled into the work station to see piles and piles and racks and carts full of all kinds of material.

Patrice carried another bundle to the front of the room. "Gather around, girls. Today I'm going to teach you what different fabrics are, just as with yesterday and the different colours." She straightened up and looked at all of us gathered around the front desk. "Fabrics are important in modelling. When you dress a model you need to pick the right colour to make them look good, and you need to pick the right fabric to make the outfit a success. Every little detail is important."

We excitedly handled the swatches of fabric Patrice handed around. "This is plaid. It is the pattern which gives it its name and this," she passed another swatch around, "is silk, from silk worms. You can get silk from a variety of animals, so it's a natural material."

We fingered swatch after swatch of amazing

material, and after the session was over, we were given booklets with long lists of material names and swatches.

"You're going to work over the weekend," Patrice said, folding up a piece of glorious coloured paisley, but she stopped when we groaned. "Don't worry, it won't be hard, it will be fun." We perked up at that word. "I want you all to raid your own wardrobes and closets and compare the clothes you own with the material information in the book." We glanced at each other excitedly. "Write down a list of what your clothes are made of so you can understand your style, and what types of material you prefer to wear. Check out magazines and websites to get an idea about what you *might like* to wear. Other than that," she said as she picked up another bundle of fabric, "go and enjoy your weekend."

After saying goodbye, we raced outside and got in the car. "Mum, can we go shopping for clothes this weekend?" Macy asked.

"Macy, we just went shopping last month for your summer wardrobe."

"I know, but Patrice wants us to go through our closets and look at what we wear and if we need anything."

"Then you can wait until it's time to buy your autumn wardrobe."

Macy mumbled, "Can I at least go to Dell's this afternoon?"

"Sorry, Macy. You've got chores, and then we've got soccer practice."

Macy and I rolled our eyes at each other. I was so glad I didn't have any brothers or sisters to deal with, but after being dropped off, I raced home to do my own chores.

*****

Macy and I spent the weekend poring through our closets and taking pictures of our favourite outfits. We learned what materials they were made of, and I figured out if the colours suited us or not. We made lots of lists and were armed with them Monday morning when we ran into the modelling school.

I skidded to a halt when I saw them.

Twenty-five mannequins were all back where they originally were.

"No," I whispered as all my fears came back in one fell swoop. "No."

"Whoa, Dell." Macy stared, wide-eyed. "They're back and they're gonna get you. Boo! Mwa ha ha…" She wiggled her fingers in my face.

I slapped Macy's evil hands away. "Don't mock me," I cried. "It's not funny. There is something seriously weird about these dummies and they're freaking me out."

"Girls," Patrice called from down the hall. "Class is starting."

Trying to focus on the door I ran down the hall and into the room on the right.

"Whoa," Macy said again. "This is huge."

We stared at the massive room, with its catwalk

down the middle, elevated five feet up from the floor, chairs lined up in rows on both sides, and floor-to-ceiling windows running the full length of the wall facing the street.

"Sit down, girls, today's lesson is about etiquette, how to sit, stand and act."

I tried desperately to listen to Patrice and follow the rules of sitting and standing when it came to being a model, but the weirds just wouldn't go. When class was over I stood rooted to the spot, willing myself to move. But I couldn't. I couldn't get my feet to move toward the door.

"Come on, Dell, we have to go," Macy called as she walked through the doorway.

I willed my feet to move, and miraculously they did. Slowly, surely, shuffling toward the door and into the hallway. My heart pounded in my chest so hard I thought it would jump out of my skin and bounce down the hall. "Just breathe, Dell. They're just dummies," I said quietly. As my right foot stepped in front of my left the hallway lights went out. "Oh, oh, oh," my breath came out in shaky gasps. I forced my left foot in front of my right as coloured lights came on, casting shadows and shapes up and down the long corridor. "Oh, oh, oh," I gasped, forcing my right foot forward.

"Dell…" came the whisper.

"Mace?" came out in a squeak. "That you?" My left foot went forward. I felt the trickles of sweat slip down my spine, and from my brow to my jawline. "Are you hiding, Mace?"

My head swung from side to side in a blind panic. The lights started spinning, my head started spinning, *I* started spinning…

Everything went black.

"Dell, Dell, can you hear me? Dell, it's Mrs Compton. Dell, wake up."

My eyes fluttered open and my vision slowly cleared.

"Oh, thank goodness." I saw Mrs C sit back. "You had us all worried, Dell. You fainted."

"Fainted," I muttered and tried to sit up. "I fainted?"

"Yes, dear," Patrice replied, standing at my feet while I lay on the floor. "You fainted in the hallway. We carried you into the lobby."

I looked around to see Macy on my right, Mrs C on my left, and Samantha, the receptionist, coming to stand behind Patrice.

"I brought you a cold drink."

She handed me a cup of cold water and I sculled it down and licked my lips. "That's good."

"Come on, Dell," Mrs C said, standing. "Better get you home." She and Macy helped me stand and walked me out to the car.

"Feeling better?" Macy asked. "You look better." She locked in her seatbelt.

I did mine up and frowned, noticing Patrice watching from the top floor as she had last week. "Yeah, feeling better."

We stopped at a burger shop to get something to eat, and then cycled to the park when we got home.

"So how come you fainted? That's not like you." Macy pumped her legs to make the swing go higher.

I just sat there rocking back and forth lost in thought.

"Dell? Dell?"

"Mmm?"

Macy slid to a halt. "Don't tell me you got spooked again?"

I looked at her. "It's not funny, Mace. Those things really freak me out, and all you can do is make fun of me. That's not being a friend." I stormed over to the grassy knoll our bikes were lying on and threw myself down next to them.

Macy came over and sat next to me. "You're right. I shouldn't make fun of you, but this is so ridiculous, Dell. You don't get scared by anything, yet you're scared of a pack of dummies." She picked a few blades of grass and pulled them apart. "What happened today? Did you not eat breakfast?"

"I *did* eat breakfast," I mumbled, not sure if I should even tell her after all her teasing.

"Then *what* happened? Come on, tell me. I'm supposed to be your best friend."

With a sigh I told her what had happened.

"They spoke to you? Asked you to help them?" Macy queried disbelievingly.

"If you're not going to believe me then you can finish the course on your own. I quit." I grabbed my bike and pedalled furiously down the street. I stormed inside my own home, ran upstairs, threw myself on the bed and burst into tears.

*****

"Dell…help us…help us, Dell…"

"No, no, go away."

"Help us, Dell…help us…"

I frantically ran down the hallway at Top Modelistè, but all I did was run, and run, and run. "Where's the door?" I cried. "I can't find the door. Let me out."

I kept on running.

"Help us, Dell…"

Long plastic-looking hands and arms reached for me, tangling in my hair, grabbing at my clothes. "Help us, Dell…help us."

CHAPTER FIVE

After having that horrible dream I *really* didn't want to go back to Top Modelistè, and I *really* didn't want to see Macy who'd called all night, and I *really* didn't want to see those awful mannequins. But Macy's mum was the one doing all the driving, so I had to climb in the car that morning. "Morning, Mrs C," I mumbled.

"Hi, Dell. Sleep well? Macy was out like a light," she replied.

I gave Macy a dirty look and at least she had the decency to look hurt. "It was all right."

"Bad dream?" Macy asked.

"Like you care," I muttered and crossed my arms over my chest. I didn't say anything for the rest of the trip and felt my heart lurch to the bottom of my stomach when we pulled to a stop outside the agency.

"Come on, Dell, let's go in together." Macy squeezed my hand and I bit my lip to stop from crying.

We walked slowly up the path and into the

building, walked slowly through the lobby and to the door that led to the hallway.

The hallway of doom!

I squeezed my eyes shut, took a deep breath and felt Macy grab my hand. I looked at her and she smiled.

"Together," she said, and led me down the hall.

I tried not to look, but the fear drove me to do it. Behind half-hooded eyes, I peeked at each mannequin. All were in the same spot as yesterday. All were unmoving. All had hands on their hips or above their head.

We made it to the runway and sat down. My breath came out in a long whoosh and then I jumped out of my skin as the door slammed behind us. We all gasped and spun around.

"Just me girls." Patrice walked to the front of the room. "Today we're going to pick out your outfits for the graduation parade, because for the next two days you're going to be practising your walk, and then on Friday we will have the full rehearsal." She pointed to the back of the room at racks of clothes none of us had noticed. "Go pick out your outfits."

We jumped up in delight, raced back, and tore through the racks looking for the latest item to wear.

After four hours I had completely forgotten about my fears, but had three different outfits to wear for the parade on Sunday.

"They look good, Dell." Macy pinned her name to one of the sets of clothes. It was something we all had to do so we remembered who had what.

"So do yours, Mace. I can't wait until Sunday." I hung my clothes on the rack.

"Neither can I. The parade will be awesome."

"I meant because this nightmare will be over," I said softly, shuffling closer to her so only she would hear.

Macy stared at me and sighed. "Has this really been that bad for you?"

I looked her square in the eye. "Yes, Mace, it has been."

"All right, girls, you can go if you've finished hanging your clothes." Patrice walked across the room toward us. "Dell dear, are you feeling better today? No more fainting spells I hope?" She stopped beside us and peered at me, as though she was peering through my soul. Her eyes examined every bit of my face. "Yes…you look okay," she said softly.

I felt my skin crawl. You know, that creepy feeling you get when something not very nice is happening?

"I'm fine, Patrice." I grabbed Macy's hand. "We'd better go." I felt her eyes watching me as we left the room. I didn't even notice we'd walked five steps before I stopped and gasped. My hand extended shakily. "Mace…" came out in a whisper. "Look, they've moved."

We looked up and down the hallway at the twenty-five mannequins. All had changed position. All had their arms outstretched. All were reaching toward me…just like in my dream…

"Mah, mah, Macy…"

She turned and looked quizzically at me. "*What now?*"

"Look." I pointed. "They've moved. They weren't like that before. Now they're all…pointing at me…arms outstretched."

"Let's get out of here," Macy said, pulling me after her.

We didn't speak of it until we got to the park on our bikes. I sat on the ground in the sun, shaking like crazy, pulling my coat around me tighter and tighter.

"Seriously, Dell," Macy said. "You need to get a grip. Someone changed the arms of the mannequins. They're *not* haunted, *not* possessed, *not* out to get you. Someone moved their arms. Plain and simple."

I looked at her in desperation. "They're freaking me out, that's what they're doing."

She nodded. "I get how they could be, but none of the rest of us is scared or having nightmares." She plucked a couple of daisies and started making a chain. "So why's it just you?"

I shook my head and the shake went through the rest of my body. "I don't know." My insides quivered and I burst into tears. "I don't know, Mace. What's wrong with me? What's wrong with me?"

She put her arm around my shoulders. "I don't know, Dell. Maybe it's some deep-seated or buried fear. Maybe you should tackle it head on and ignore them."

I sniffled and wiped my face. "Ignore them? How?"

She shrugged. "I don't know. March in there tomorrow and ignore them." She linked her arm through mine. "I've never seen you so scared of anything, Dell, but this has got you frightened out of your skin. So we're going to march in there tomorrow, side by side, and completely ignore them. Deal?"

I grinned, instantly feeling better. "Deal!"

*****

And that's what happened Wednesday morning. Macy and I stood arm in arm in the lobby, looked at each other, nodded, and looking straight ahead, marched down the long glossy red hallway. We marched into the runway room, did our catwalk practice, and four hours later marched back out the door.

"Well?" Macy asked later in the park. "How was it?"

I shook my head in amazement. "It worked, Mace. It really worked. I was so scared and all, but I didn't see them move, didn't hear them call my name or call for help. I didn't see or hear anything."

"Good! Now, all we have to do is do that again tomorrow and Friday, then get through Sunday and we're free from the *Top Modelistè* modelling and etiquette course."

I took a deep breath and slowly let it out. "Yep." I nodded. "Just gotta get through three more days."

*****

On Thursday morning we did the same thing. Marched our way along the hallway and into the runway room, practised our walk, and getting in and out of our three outfits and marched back out when it was over.

If only every day had been so easy.

CHAPTER SIX

And Friday morning started that way too.

We marched inside, down the hall and into the runway room, to find it had been rearranged. No longer were the chairs in rows on both sides of the catwalk, but now they surrounded round tables with nice white tablecloths.

"Wow," I breathed. "Must be getting ready for Sunday."

Patrice came into the room and clapped her hands. "Okay, girls, for the next two hours we're going to learn about table etiquette and manners and which utensils to use for which meals so that you're ready for Sunday night. Come and sit at these two tables." She waved her hands either side of her, gesturing to the tables filled with cutlery and plates.

We took our places and I glanced down to see so many knives, forks and spoons.

"When it comes to cutlery we always start from the outside and work our way to the inside." Patrice indicated to the plate in front of her. "Regardless of how many courses you have, the rule is always the same. You start with your bread knife and end with your dessert spoon."

For the next two hours I concentrated on what each item was for and how to hold and use it. From the sound of it, we'd be having three courses. I'd heard of some dinners having eight or twelve, but only in very fancy expensive restaurants or castles in European countries.

"Okay, girls. Take home your paperwork and practise at home. This will all come in handy Sunday night." Patrice smoothed her bun. "Now, we will try something a little different to see how far you've come with learning about materials and colour. I'm going to get you to put together two different outfits, and then I'll tell you the rest when you're done. The clothes are on the racks at the back of the room."

We turned and looked. "Make them as plain or extravagant as you can, but remember to use what you have been taught." She waved us off. "You've got twenty minutes."

We raced to the back of the room and grabbed bright coloured fabric. We had hats and shoes, belts and bags to choose from in all colours, materials and styles. I matched up a cute ruffled skirt in a soft red plaid with a plain short sleeved shirt and soft pink sleeveless vest. Knee high socks and buckle up shoes completed one outfit. For the other I matched a wild coloured leather hat with a velvet coat with fur trim, bell bottom jeans, a green top and funky boots.

I glanced at Macy and saw she'd done a similar

thing. One simple outfit, one crazy.

"Okay, girls, your twenty minutes are up." Patrice came over and eyed off each outfit. "Fabulous choices. Now, one last thing, to understand how to dress models for photo shoots and fashion shows and all the work that goes into it, you're going to put your outfits onto models."

Macy and I excitedly clapped our hands and looked at each other.

"However…you won't be using real-life models…"

I think my breath stopped…

"You'll be using the mannequins out in the hallway."

That's when my heart practically stopped beating and I felt the life leaving my body.

"So grab your clothes and I'll lead you to your test subjects."

Macy grabbed my hand as I stood rooted to the spot. "It's okay, Dell. You can do this," she whispered. "You can do this."

I stared at the ground feeling faint, dizzy, as though I was going to be sick.

"Dell, Macy?" Patrice came up to us. "Is everything okay? Dell, you don't look so good."

"She's not feeling very good," Macy replied. "I think maybe she needs something to eat or drink."

"Of course!" Patrice exclaimed and out of thin air came Samantha with a glass of juice and a sandwich. "You sit and eat for a few minutes then I'll show you to your mannequins. I have two very special ones for you, Dell."

I freaked out on the inside as I watched her walk into the hall. "What did she mean by that?" I furiously whispered, ramming half of the sandwich into my mouth.

"Calm down, Dell." Macy sat beside me and took a bite of the other half. "She may not mean anything by it. You need to stop letting your imagination run away with you." She picked up the glass, but I snatched it away.

"My imagination's running away with me, huh?" I drank the juice and put the glass down as Patrice came back in.

"Feeling better? Good. Grab your outfits and I'll show you to your mannequins."

"Mmm." The small sound came out of my throat, but I gulped it down and grabbed the clothes. I followed Macy into the hall and stood panic stricken at the sight before me. The mannequins had their limbs chopped off and spewed all over the floor.

Patrice must have seen my expression. "Samantha and I are helping you to remove the arms and legs or torso so you can get the clothes on more easily. Macy, you'll be dressing mannequins 2 and 3. Dell." She turned to me. "*You're* very special. You get to dress our very first graduate mannequin."

I stared in horror from the dummy to Patrice.

"And last year's winner as well. The very first and the last, Dell. You get to dress them both."

I watched her expression change and felt the temperature drop to a hundred below. I shivered. This woman scared me.

"Now," she said. "I'll show you how to remove the limbs." She firmly grabbed number 1's left arm, twisted it right, and pulled it off. I felt a pain go through my own left arm. "Ow." I dropped the clothes and rubbed my arm.

"Is everything all right, Dell?" she asked, holding the arm in her hand. Her voice was low and smooth…and scary and…and…and evil.

"Dell?" Macy popped up from behind Patrice's back. "You okay?"

I rubbed my arm some more. "Yeah, must have been holding the clothes the wrong way and got a cramp or something."

Patrice blinked. Her lids slowly slid down and up in slow motion. "I'll show you the other arm." Laying down the left, she grabbed the right, twisted, and pulled it off. "There," she said softly. "Both arms."

I gulped and she gazed down at me.

"I'll remove the torso as well, shall I?"

Holding the dummy by the waist, she twisted and lifted it off the lower half of the body. After putting it on the floor next to the arms, she stood and straightened her powder blue skirt suit. It looked like the one she wore every day.

"Now, Dell, you take the clothes off, put the new ones on, and then pop the body back together."

I rubbed my right arm, which now hurt, as well as my waist. Boy, did I feel sick.

"Once you've finished number 1, you pop down the hall and do number 25. When you're done, you take the old clothes back into the room and leave. Do you understand?" She watched me closely, peering at me with those evil eyes of hers.

I gulped and rubbed my arms once more. "Yes, ma'am, uh, Patrice."

"Good girl, Dell." She patted me on the shoulder. "Very good girl," she finished quietly before walking off, scaring the absolute bejesus out of me.

I have never been so scared in my entire life. Disaster, zombies, you name it, it didn't scare me, but not once have I ever felt so scared in real life. Now I was scared by someone so pleasant looking and by store mannequins that do nothing but come apart and wear clothes.

"Hurry up, Dell, we've got an hour left." Macy finished putting an arm on mannequin 2 and stood back. "What do you think?" She looked at me for approval.

Through feverish eyes I glanced at the dummy. "The hair's crooked, but the clothes are nice," I mumbled.

"Geez Dell, you really don't look good. You coming down with something?" She grabbed her second outfit and moved to dummy no.3.

I glanced up and down both sides of the hall. *Okay, Dell, get a grip. You can see arms and legs everywhere. They are dummies, not humans. They cannot move, or talk or walk on their own; they are dummies.*

I looked down at the parts on the floor at my feet. Two arms and a torso. Taking a deep breath to calm myself, I decided to remove the skirt first, figuring it would be easiest. After swapping it over with the one I'd chosen I looked at the shoes.

"They come off at the knee," Macy called.

I looked at her and saw her twist the calf of the left leg on her mannequin. I grabbed my dummy's right leg and twisted. My hands slid around the leg. What? I grabbed and twisted again, but the leg wouldn't come off.

"It looks like that one might be stuck." Samantha gave the dummy's knee a kick and twisted it off. "They need a bit of oil or something," she said with a sly grin.

I sped through shoe changing and ripped off the clothes on the torso. After hurriedly pulling on the clothes I'd chosen, I bent down to pick it up.

It was warm!

What!?

Probably from friction, I thought, handling it. I wrapped my arms around it, lifted, and put it onto the bottom half. I stumbled and nearly lost my grip as it started sliding, but I pushed it up and found the hole to lock it into. I jammed it in and twisted it into place, sighing in relief when it locked and stopped moving.

"Dell…help us…"

I lurched back and stumbled, falling over the arms and onto my butt. "Ow."

"Dell, you all right?"

I turned to see everyone staring at me. Everyone, including the mannequins. "Um, yeah. Just lost my footing and tripped is all." I scrambled to my feet.

Everyone went back to what they were doing, and I quickly jammed the arms into their sockets, straightened the hair, and stepped back. One down, one to go.

I scooped up the second set of clothes and raced down the hall, dumping them before ripping the arms from the torso and changing its pants and shoes. It took me a few minutes, and I fumbled getting the legs back on while it was wearing jeans.

"Dell, leave the jeans undone and around the ankles while you put the legs back," Patrice said from beside me.

"Ah." I stumbled back. I was scared enough as is, but her silently popping up beside me was eerie.

"Put the legs on then pull the jeans up." She looked down at me. "It's easier."

I gulped, undid the jeans and rammed the legs in. I saw the others collecting the old clothes to take back into the room and quickly pulled the jeans up. I yanked off the top and put the new one on, then threw the velvet coat over it. I picked up an arm and shoved it up the sleeves and into its socket. I added the other one and got ready to pick the torso up.

"Bye, Patrice," some of the girls said as they walked past me.

"Girls, see you Sunday," she replied from her position on the other side of the hall.

In a panic that I'd be the only one left, I heaved the torso up and onto the legs. Fumbling, stumbling, I finally managed to get it in and locked.

"Meet you outside, Dell." Macy ran past.

"Mace, wait," I called, going into Mach 1000 panic mode.

"You're nearly finished, Dell, you won't be long." Patrice seemed to glide past me, her eyes burning into mine. "It won't be long at all."

"Uh, ah." I turned to the dummy and adjusted its hair, rammed the hat on and fixed the clothes. With speed to match an Olympic runner, I grabbed the old clothes, sped into the runway room, and back out into the hallway.

The hallway was now dark.

The hallway now had twenty-five mannequins reaching out their arms to me…

CHAPTER SEVEN

Coloured lights clicked on one by one down the hall. They moved, swirled and spun around.

"Help us…help us, Dell…"

"Argh," I cried. "You're not real. You're not real." I burst into tears. "Leave me alone, you're not real."

"Help us, Dell…"

Twenty-five heads turned in my direction.

"Help us…"

"No, what do you want? Leave me alone!"

Twenty-five sets of arms moved in my direction.

"Set us free, Dell…set us free…"

"Why are you doing this to me? Leave me alone. Leave me alone." My feet finally managed to find the power to move and I managed to make it down the hall, out the front door and to Mrs C's car.

"Take me home," I cried, buckling myself in.

"Dell! What happened? Did someone do something to you? I have a right mind to—"

"Just take me home please," I managed through my tears and huddled against the door as Macy sat watching me. Mrs C dropped me off at my house then took Macy home. I ran upstairs into my room and hid in my bed for the rest of the day.

*****

"Dell?" my mum called through the door. "I brought you some soup."

I heard the door open and something being placed on my bedside table.

"Dell?" She pulled back the quilt and sat beside me, touching her hand to my forehead then my cheek. "You feel a little warm, probably from hiding under your quilt on a warm summer's day. It's six o'clock. I brought you some soup and a bread roll." She stared at me intently and I tried to hide under my pillow. "Dell." She removed it. "Mrs Compton called and told me what happened. From the look of your face I'd say you've been crying ever since. So…" She handed me a small bottle of juice. "Have a drink and tell me, *in your own words*, what happened."

I sat up against the wall and thirstily drank the juice till it was gone. I burped.

"Dell!"

I giggled. "Scuse me."

"So, what's wrong?" She sat beside me with a pillow behind her.

I looked down at my lap. "I'm going crazy. Are there crazy people in our family that I don't know about? You know, the ones that went cuckoo and need to go away to mental homes?" I asked hopefully.

She laughed. My mum always thought I was

being funny even when I was serious. "No, Dell, there are no crazy people in our family."

"Then why am I going crazy?"

"Are you?" She looked at me seriously. "What makes *you* think you are?"

I sighed and felt what little energy I had left leave my body. "Because I keep thinking the mannequins in the hallway are talking to me, asking me for help, and they change positions. Their arms always reach for me and try and grab me. But they aren't. Are they?"

"Who said they aren't?"

I looked up in surprise. My mum looked dead serious.

"What?"

"Who said they aren't moving, or asking you for help?"

"Well," I started. "Macy never sees them or hears them, and she's been making jokes about it since I first told her."

"Macy's not special like you, Dell."

"You're just trying to make me feel better." I glanced around my room at the fluffy toys, overflowing bookshelves, and desk.

"I'm serious, Dell. Macy's not special like you; she doesn't have special people in her family."

"Special people?" I searched her face for answers or even a joke about to break. "What do you mean *special* people?"

"I mean special people who can *see* special things, and *do* special things, and *hear* special things no one else can." She brushed my hair off my forehead. "You're special, Dell, with special abilities you're clearly starting to experience. It generally happens around twelve."

"What does?"

She leaned close. "The ability to hear and see things; things that are not real or no longer living." She got up from the bed. "I told Macy she can't come until tomorrow afternoon. I want the two of you to go have some fun before this is over on Sunday." She grabbed the door handle. "Dessert's in the fridge when you're ready." She disappeared behind the door.

*****

"She said what?" Macy asked Saturday afternoon. "That you can see and hear things no one else can? What did she mean?" She was lying on her stomach on my huge flower rug, feet swinging in the air, a magazine and a bowl of cherries in front of her.

"I don't know." I was sitting at my desk. "But I thought I'd try and find out by looking for stuff online." I tapped a few keys and clicked the mouse. "Whoa."

"What?"

"I see dead people!"

Macy jumped up and stood beside me. "What do you *mean* you see dead people? Your life is *not* a movie, you know!" She peered over my shoulder at the computer.

"But what if I do? Look." I pointed to the screen. "People that can hear and see things no one else can are called psychics and mediums. They can pick up on people who have died."

"Psychics and mediums," Macy scoffed and crossed her arms. "My mum said that's a load of hooey. There's no such thing."

"But what if there is?" I excitedly looked at her. "What if it runs in my family?"

"Or maybe your mum was just being polite when she told you there were no crazies in the family. She told you you were special just to make you feel better." She picked up the bowl of cherries and sat on the bed.

Now I felt terrible because what Macy was saying was mean and hurtful. "My mum *never* lies to me, Mace, and I know when she's trying to make me feel better. She was dead serious." I spun around in my desk chair.

Macy sighed. "Then what you're saying is that those twenty-five mannequins in the hallway at *Top Modelistè* are what? Haunted? Possessed? Invaded by aliens?" A cocky expression covered her face.

"I can definitely tell when *you're trying* to be funny," I mumbled, "because you never are. Your jokes suck."

Her face fell and she scowled. "Thanks ever so much."

"You're welcome," I replied and went back to the computer.

"What will you do tomorrow then?"

Now it was my turn to sigh. I didn't want to walk back down that hallway again, but we had one last day before it was over. "I don't know. Maybe what we've done for the last few times. March in there and ignore them." I felt my brows go up. "Or maybe, now that I have a special talent, I could walk in there and ask them what they want and what help they need?" Macy rolled her eyes. "Maybe I'll become a psychic detective and track down possessed mannequins to help them." I gazed up at my ceiling at the hundreds of coloured star stickers. "And maybe, I'll visit a galaxy far far away and send them home."

"Bahahahaha." Macy rolled around on my bed holding her stomach. "You really *are* cuckoo. Bahahahaha!"

CHAPTER EIGHT

Sunday morning at ten, we got out of the car and stood on the pavement facing Top Modelistè. I gulped.

"Don't tell me you're scared again," Macy teased. "I thought you were going to use your new found psychic abilities to talk to them?"

I gave her a half-hearted grin through gritted teeth. "So did I."

She rolled her eyes and laughed. "Come on, let's go." Dragging me up to the front door she stopped when she saw the sign. "Oh, no."

I banged into her. "Oh, what?" I clamped my eyes shut. "Has it been cancelled? Please say it's been cancelled. Please, please, please."

"Bahahaha. You'd like that wouldn't you? No. Open your eyes."

I peeked at her under a half-hooded eyelid.

"It's not been cancelled, we just have to go round back and use that door."

I took her words in and my eyes flew open, but my shoulders sagged. "Oh, well then. That's all right.

Which way?"

We checked the sign and walked around the right side of the building, past the car park, and to the huge double doors at the back.

"Girls," Samantha called. "You're the last ones to arrive. Go inside."

We ran into the huge room we'd be having our parade in, and saw it was crowded with people checking lights, and turning music on and off, putting cloths and cutlery on tables, and hanging decorations.

"Whoa." I looked around in stunned amazement.

"Girls," Patrice called. "Please go backstage and I will be with you in a minute."

We drifted through the door that led to the huge area behind the runway. People were scurrying around there too. We saw a hairdressing stand, a make-up table, and an area for taking photos all set up.

"Whoa," came out of my mouth again. "This is so cool."

"I can't believe we've done this," Macy said from beside me. "Who knew we'd actually win and get to do the two week course, and now here we are at graduation. We get our hair done, our make-up done, *and* free photographs."

"Okay, girls, listen up and gather around." We excitedly assembled around Patrice. "We are going to do a walkthrough just so the light technicians and music director can get the right look and sound happening. That means you get changed into your first outfits and line up in order. Did you all study the rundown sheet you were given?"

"Yes."

"Then you know what order you're in." She pointed to the dressing screens behind against the wall. "Your names are in position with your clothes, so please go and change into outfit number one."

We hurried off and quickly changed while listening to the music pouring in from the main room. When we were ready, we lined up and waited to be called.

Samantha came over to us, looking at her clipboard. "I will be directing you onto the stage. You will walk down to the end with a few twirls in the middle, and then come back and get changed into your second outfit. Then we'll start again."

"Are they ready?" cackled over the walkie-talkie on Samantha's belt.

"They are. Okay, number one, get ready." She waited until Patrice made some introductions and then the music started. "And…go."

A blonde girl of fifteen went first and strangely, here we were on graduation day and I still didn't know their names. Macy and I held onto each other in excitement as we waited for our turn, barely letting go long enough to go out on the catwalk.

We did it again for the next two outfits with Patrice talking in between and while we were on stage. She let the imaginary crowd know who we were, how old we are, and how well we'd done during the course. When it was over we took a breather.

"Well done, girls." Patrice came backstage to see us. "Take a break and go out and get some sun. There's a small catering truck out there with lunch, and then we'll do it again. And don't forget to change into your normal clothes so you don't get these outfits dirty."

We changed and ran outside to a small truck with its side up. "Hello girls, we've got sandwiches, fruit and water."

We grabbed one of each and went and sat on the grassy lawn at the back of the car park.

"Gosh that was scary," Macy said around a mouthful of ham sandwich.

"Yeah," I mumbled around my chicken one. "It was."

"And I can't believe we get to keep the clothes we picked to model." Macy slurped some water down. "That is even cooler."

"I know, and they're *expensive* clothes. I saw the skirt I picked in a catalogue. My mum would have a fit if I asked for it."

"That's why I picked that awesome coat." Macy took a bite of banana. "Because I would *never* get something like that, not even for birthday or Christmas."

"Girls." Samantha walked into the car park. "Time for the second rehearsal."

We dropped our rubbish in a nearby bin and hurried inside. Fifteen minutes later, we'd changed back into our first outfits and were walking down the runway.

"Dell…go." Samantha prodded me.

I climbed the stairs, stood in the middle of the runway, posed with my hands on my hips, and then casually walked toward Patrice who was standing at the end. The music thumped and the lights flashed, and I did a little twirl before stopping at the end. I walked back the way I'd come and left the stage, high-fiving Macy as we passed. I changed into my second set of clothes and lined up. There were five girls before us and five after us, so we had to wait awhile before going on stage again. We chatted amongst ourselves about tonight and what our parents would think.

It was my turn again, and down the catwalk I sashayed. I twirled and stopped, distracted by something at the door to the hallway.

"Dell, dear, keep moving. Don't let yourself be distracted," Patrice called sharply. "Keep in time with the music."

With my heart racing I walked back and fell down the stairs.

"Hey, Dell, take it easy," Macy grumbled. "You nearly knocked me over."

She raced up the stairs and took off down the runway.

"Are you all right, Dell?" Samantha asked.

I looked up from my position on the ground to see my fellow graduates smirking at me. "Yeah." I brushed my hands off and struggled to my feet. "I just tripped, I'm fine."

"All right, go and change and line up again."

I made it to my change station with Macy hot on my tail.

"What happened to you?

I pulled on another top. "Yeah, sorry. I tripped down the stairs."

"So I noticed. Glad you didn't knock me over," she mumbled under her clothes. "Are you all right, not bleeding or anything?"

I checked my knees which I'd fallen on. "A bit sore, but no blood." I changed into my jeans and finished dressing.

On my way down the runway for the third and last time, I glanced at the doorway. I couldn't see anyone going in or out, but I did see a figure standing there watching, arms outstretched, wearing the clothes I'd put on it yesterday.

Mannequin number 25 was standing in the doorway…

CHAPTER NINE

I screamed…

The music stopped…

The lights stopped…

Everybody stopped…

"Dell," Patrice said from the floor in front of me. "Why did you scream, dear?"

I panicked, licked my lips, and swung my head back and forth. "Um, oh," I panted. "Um, sorry. My knees um, they really hurt from before when I fell off the stage." I leant down and rubbed them. "I must have turned the wrong way and pain shot through them. Sorry." I glanced down in embarrassment, feeling my face get hotter and hotter.

"Go backstage and get an ice pack from the caterers. Leave it on for fifteen minutes," Patrice replied coolly. "Wait for the music to come back on and pick up where you left off. Is that understood?"

"Yes, Patrice," I mumbled, unable to look at her or anyone else.

The music started again and I limped off stage. Macy gave me a filthy look as she went out for her turn.

"Change your clothes before you get that ice pack," Samantha added curtly.

"Okay." I felt daggers from the other girls and couldn't wait for it to be over.

*****

"What *was* that?" Macy asked when she called me later. We were at home resting up before going back for the parade.

I sighed. There was no point telling her especially since it was nearly over. "My knees really hurt is all. I must have pulled something when I turned."

"How are they now?"

I examined them and gave them a poke. "Sore. A little red, might be bruised later."

"Serves you right for not looking where you're going. Gotta go, see you tonight."

*****

It was all a blur of excitement and coloured lights when we arrived backstage, ready to walk the walk down the runway in front of family and friends.

"Dell, you're up next," Samantha told me, and I nervously stood to the side of the stairs. Moments later, it was my turn. I stood on the catwalk and posed before strutting my stuff. I saw people left and right of me, my family on my left applauding. I came to the end and turned before walking back and down the stairs.

Twenty minutes later I did it again.

Patrice's voice came over the loudspeaker. "Say hello to Delany Chester, one of two winners of this year's competition. She likes to go by the nickname, Dell, and is twelve-years-old."

I stopped and turned.

"She loves disaster movies, but is scared of mannequins."

"What!" I tripped over my own feet, but kept going while the crowd laughed behind my back. "Why did she say that," I cried to Macy when she took my place. I was on the verge of tears that Patrice could humiliate me in such a way, so I took my time getting changed.

"I thought it was funny." Macy popped up beside me to change.

"It…it wasn't." My voice broke.

"Dell?" Macy peered over the divider. "Don't cry, you can't cry now. We have another round to do and you'll ruin your make-up."

"It was mean and horrible and so embarrassing," I sobbed.

Macy quickly grabbed tissues and wiped my face. "Get changed and get your make-up fixed, you don't have time for this."

I stopped crying at her take-charge tone and finished dressing. I got the make-up lady to fix the mess I'd created before heading out for the last parade. When I came offstage, I had a bunch of photos taken as a reminder of the course and graduation evening.

Once the parade was over, we went to have dinner

with our families and sat listening to a video of all the stars that had come to *Top Modelistè* modelling agency. When the meal was over, we excitedly watched Patrice take the stage.

"Ladies and gentlemen, we are very proud of your daughters. They have learned a lot and come a long way in two weeks. There are many prizes as well. All of the girls get to take home all three outfits, and a set of free photographs from tonight."

I glanced over at Mum and saw her proud expression.

"There will be three winners, first, second and third. I will start with the third contestant." She paused to open the envelope she was holding. "Third place receives a five hundred dollar gift card from *Denny's Department Store* and it is... Destiny Robards..."

I heard squealing coming from the other side of the room, and looked over at Macy who was with her family at the next table and grinned.

We watched Destiny collect her prize, put on her sash, and do a strut down the catwalk. When she left, Patrice spoke again.

"Second place will receive a *one thousand* dollar gift card from *Denny's Department Store*, and a one year's subscription to *Top Modelistè Magazine*." She opened the envelope. "First runner up is...London Richards..."

Macy and I exchanged a puzzled glance as we watched her go on stage. Did they all have weird names?

"And now..." Patrice held up the third and final envelope. The music died down and the lights stopped flashing. "The winner, and brand new graduate of the *Top Modelistè Modelling and Etiquette* course, taking home a *two thousand* dollar gift card from *Denny's Department Store*, a one year subscription to *Top Modelistè Magazine, plus,* a year-long free course certificate for her and a friend to any of our other courses held in the next year is..."

CHAPTER TEN

I sat riveted to my seat.

"Delany Chester..."

What!?

Macy screamed and jumped up and hugged me. My mum and dad did the same. Everyone was cheering and clapping, and Macy pushed me toward the stage.

I moved one foot at a time, not believing it was real. It couldn't possibly be happening? *No, not to me!* I climbed the stairs and walked over to Patrice, shook her hand, accepted the certificates, put on my sash, and slowly walked down the catwalk for the final time. I made it back to Patrice.

"Dell, dear," she said quietly in my ear while we posed for photos on stage. "I need you and your parents to come to my office to sign some paperwork. I'll come and get you in a few minutes." I looked at her in a daze and left the stage.

"Oh, my gosh, Dell," Macy squealed when I got back to the table. She hugged me tight and we bounced around in circles. "You won, you won.

That means we can go on a shopping spree to Denny's. We can get clothes and shoes and bags and jewellery—"

I stopped jumping. "What do you mean *we?* That gift card will last me ages, and besides, you got your outfits for free just like I did."

Her face crumpled. "You mean…you mean you're not going to share with me?"

I knew Macy's guilt trip tactics when I saw them. "Macy, you get to do all the courses here, but you *don't* get my shopping spree."

A few of the other girls came over and congratulated me, but most of them didn't bother. I saw Patrice come over to speak to my parents and they looked in my direction, waving me over. "Gotta go," I said. "Mum and Dad have to sign some papers or something."

"All right, we'll wait," Macy called out behind me.

I followed Mum, Dad and Patrice out the door to the hallway before realising what was happening. I was about to freak out when I saw the mannequins weren't even there. *That's strange,* I thought. We walked into the lobby, up the stairs, and into her office.

"Mr and Mrs Chester, we are so proud of Dell. She's come a long way in two weeks." Patrice indicated to two chairs. "Please be seated."

I looked around the lushly decorated room.

"Yes, Ms Pellcott, so are we," Mum replied, seating herself.

"I just have some papers for you to sign to say

that Dell received her prizes, and we are in no way responsible for loss or damage." She brought out a stack of papers from her desk drawer and handed them over, with a gold pen, to Mum and Dad to sign.

They whipped their signatures across the papers and handed them back.

"Good, now Samantha will escort you out while I have a quick word with Dell. She'll meet you downstairs." She pointed toward the door where I saw Samantha magically appear.

"This way please," Samantha said, holding the door open.

I frowned and saw Mum and Dad think it was weird too.

"I don't think—" Mum started.

"We'll just be a moment," Patrice coolly cut in. "Please wait downstairs."

I was feeling scared now. Those icy cold tendrils of fear and unknowing silently crept their way through my body.

My mother was unconvinced, and the expression on her face said a few different things. Reluctantly, after exchanging looks, my parents left the room.

Patrice turned to me. "Please come with me, Dell." She opened a door to the left of her desk. "This way."

I was really scared now. I didn't know what she was about to do or what was about to happen. And really, what *could I* do about it?

"*This way, Dell.*" She waited for me.

With fear in my heart, I followed. Followed her

down a narrow flight of stairs, and along an even narrower corridor. "Where are we going?" Fear shook my voice. "What's going on?"

"What's going on is that you know too much, Dell." She opened a door and waited. "Down this way."

I followed her down another flight of stairs, narrower than the first, but this one was dark and dank. "What do you mean, know too much? What do I know?"

We reached the bottom and stopped. Patrice turned to me and stared with eyes of ice. "You know, don't you, Dell?"

I. Was. So. Scared…

I gulped. "Know what? I want my Mum and Dad. I want to go." I turned to go back upstairs, but she grabbed my arm in a vice-like grip and slammed the door. "Ah!"

"You know about the mannequins, don't you know, Dell," she screeched.

I burst into tears. "Know what?" I sobbed. "I don't know what you're talking about. I want my mum and dad."

She dragged me along another corridor. "Well, *you're not getting* your mummy and daddy because they just signed you over to me."

"What?" I struggled to get out of her grasp. "You're hurting me. I want my mummy and daddy. Stop it, Patrice, please, you're hurting me."

"They're not your mummy and daddy anymore. Those papers they just signed meant they signed you over to me. I now *own* you.'" She leaned in close, her eyes piercing through my soul. I think I wet myself. "You are *mine* now, Dell. Your family will forget about you, and your friend Macy will find another girl to play with. *I...own...you.*"

I withered under her stare and didn't have the strength or will to fight.

Patrice dragged me into another room and shoved me onto the floor where I lay sprawled. "Take a good look around, Dell. This is your last day on Earth."

I looked around. I think it was a basement or something with a concrete floor, sheets of metal on the walls, and chains hanging from the roof. It was dark and stinky, and red lights mixed with yellow ones casting an eerie glow around the room. Twenty-five mannequins surrounded a large pool of bubbling water that steamed merrily away. I frantically looked around.

"There's no way out, Dell. You're about to join your fellow winners."

"I don't understand," I wailed, glancing at each dummy. "What's going on?"

She kicked me and I yelped. "What's going on, you stupid little girl, is that you heard them. They tried reaching out to you to help them. But all it did was freak you out." She waved her arms out. "These are the winners of the *Top Modelistè* agency for the past twenty-five years. Each girl, sadly, learned the secret so they *had* to win." She looked down. "*They had* to win so I could take ownership of them and keep them from telling my secret."

I rubbed my hands over my face frantically to wipe away my tears. "What…what secret?" I whispered.

Patrice's face twisted into anger. "The secret to making real-life mannequins. Dummies that look *so* real you'll think they *are* real." The laugh that rang out around the room was pure evil. Not that I know what pure evil sounds like. *"Because they are."*

"Help us, Dell…help us," I heard and turned to see them reaching out their hands to me. I screamed and scurried backwards.

Patrice spun around. "That's right, Dell. They look real because they *are* real. Real-life human beings dipped in a resin wax mix. Real-life *human dummies*. And *you*," her voice boomed, "Delany Jane Chester, *you* are about to join them."

"No," I whimpered. "No." I struggled to my feet, but Patrice grabbed my arm.

"Congratulations, Delany Jane Chester, *you* are the Next Top Mannequin!"

EPILOGUE

One Year Later

I was cold and lonely, and had been standing for ages when the overhead lights flickered on and voices rang out from another room.

"Okay, girls," Patrice called. "Follow me." She breezed past with a group of girls trailing behind her. "All of our past winners are on the wall in front of you. They've all gone on to bigger and better things."

Two girls stopped in front of me.

"Delany Jane Chester," one whispered. "I've never heard of her."

"Neither have I," the other said. "All the plaque says is she won last year's modelling course."

"Wow, look at her eyes." The first girl moved closer. "They look *so* real."

"Yeah," the second girl replied. "They do."

I moved my eyes so I could look straight at them. "Help me…" I whispered. "Help me…"

Their eyes widened in horror, their mouths opened in fear…

"Help me…"

CINDERFELLA AND PRINCESS CHARMING: WITCH HUNTERS

CHAPTER ONE

"Oh, Cinderfella, I want you to know I will be marrying the woman I have been seeing, tomorrow, in a short ceremony at the church in town."

Cinderfella looked up in surprise at the words, and his hands stopped polishing the wooden staff he was cradling in his lap. "Father?"

Baron Von Duty moved to his son's side and placed a hand on his shoulder. "I know this will be hard for you, Cinderfella, but I need a mother for you and a companion for myself. I'm not young anymore, even though you are." He walked around the table and stood staring at his son. "You need to be taken care of. I've been ill, of late, and it won't do you any good to be alone if anything happens to me. So, after seeing Madame Neila for some months now, ah…she's a widow with two sons…we have decided to marry for both of our conveniences." He waited for his son's reply, unsure of how he would react.

Cinderfella shook his head slowly, his hands closing around the staff, his fingers turning white with anger. "Father, we have been fine on our own. I'm almost sixteen and can look after myself. I've been running the stables for two years now."

The Baron put up a hand to stop him. "And you've done a fine job, Cinderfella, but it is done. We will marry tomorrow, and I hope you will be there to welcome Madame and her sons with open arms, but I will understand if you cannot." He walked back around the table and squeezed his son's shoulder. "They will be moving in with us as well. There are more than enough rooms to go around, so you will not need to move out of yours." He walked toward the door with the gait of an old man near his end, pausing only long enough to give a hacking cough. "I will see you tomorrow, Cinderfella." He closed the door behind him.

Cinderfella shook with fury. A woman! Married! *How could he consider such a thing after Mother passed? How could he dare to take another to his home? And a woman with sons! Like I need brothers! I've been fine on my own.*

His eyes bulged with hatred as he glared around the tack room. The stable was a large part of the Von Duty estate and it was his job to keep it running in tip-top shape. What would happen now there would be a woman on the estate? He stalked the handmade dummy figure he'd made up for practising his martial arts, and whipping around in a circle, he swung his staff back and forth and bashed the dummy until it split in two.

He straightened and stared at the two pieces of

hay-filled chaff sack on the floor as his heart slowed down to normal speed. *If you so much as hurt my father, that is what I will do to you, Madame Neila.*

*****

"I now pronounce you, husband and wife."

The small group gathered in the church politely applauded as Baron Von Duty kissed his newly married Baroness Von Duty.

Cinderfella leaned against the back wall watching with a grim expression as two handsome young men stood to kiss and congratulate the Baroness, and solemnly shake his father's hand. *Must be my new stepbrothers,* he thought, straightening as his father and new stepmother walked down the aisle toward him with the young men trailing behind.

"Cinderfella, I'm so glad you came," the Baron cheered. "Come, meet your new mother, Baroness Von Duty."

She politely extended her hand for him to kiss, and he politely kissed it in return. She glowed with youth and radiance and some distaste at having a stepson.

A lot more youth than my father, Cinder thought. *She looks way too young to have two sons older than me.*

"And these are your new stepbrothers, Wilhelm and Mikhale."

Cinder extended his hand to shake. They glared down at it with such screwed up faces that Cinder thought they would be sick. Standing there with his hand out, he noticed the Baroness give them a slight nod, and they both accepted his hand.

"Nice to meet you," they muttered before retracting their hands and wiping them in stiff white handkerchiefs.

The other guests came up and congratulated the Baron and his new wife, and they all retreated to the Von Duty estate for the celebration. The Baron had spared no expense for the wedding reception. Maids handed out food and drink while the Baron regaled his guests with the story of how he met his new wife. Cinder retreated to the stables not long after.

Holding his staff in his hand, he slowly turned it over, marvelling at the hours it must have taken to craft such workmanship. He swung it around over his head and executed a few back spins. He had been practising martial arts since turning ten, and was almost an expert after training with one of the country's master martial artists.

"Oh, look, Cinderfella thinks he can actually *use* that thing!"

With hairs prickling on the back of his neck at the voice, Cinder slowly turned to find his new stepbrothers standing in the stable doorway.

They stepped forward, almost marching in time with each other. "Little Cinderfella is no longer *single* Cinderfella," Mikhale sneered.

"Little Cinderfella now has *us* to deal with," Wilhelm added.

"Is *that* what you think?" Cinderfella added before swiftly cartwheeling and somersaulting over the ground between them. "Ha, ya, ha!" He expertly swung his staff back and forth, making them back up in fright. "You don't scare me, my dear stepbrothers. I can stand up and defend myself."

They haughtily straightened their hair and smoothed their clothes. "You may think you're good, Cinderfella, but we're good at what *we* do too," Mikhale said, backing away.

"Yeah," sneered Wilhelm. "And don't you forget it." They scurried away to the house leaving Cinderfella shaking his head in dismay.

*****

Over the next two years they got along, Cinderfella with his stepbrothers, and Cinderfella with his stepmother. Baroness Von Duty had relished her role on such a grand scale on such a grand estate that she told people what to do and how to do it. Anyone she didn't like she fired, only for the Baron to replace that person with someone else.

The Baroness also loved spending money and redecorated the house with each passing season in the finest fabrics the Baron's money could buy. The Baron didn't mind. His ailing health meant whatever joy he could get out of life was meant for the taking.

One day, Cinderfella came out of his room, and upon hearing voices, decided to stand silently in the hallway to listen to his parents' conversation. Out of curiosity, of course.

"Oh, Baron, my darling husband, how you spoil me so." Baroness Von Duty fluttered around her husband's ailing body propped up in his chair. She fluffed his pillows and straightened the blanket across his lap.

He gently reached up and grabbed a hold of her hand. "It's a pleasure, my dear. You have brought me much happiness these last two years, and you've been a good wife to me, and a good mother to my son."

Cinderfella rolled his eyes and shook his head. *Good mother, my butt!* he thought. *She all but ignores me and prefers her arrogant little brats.*

His father continued, "I am not far from leaving this world, and want you to know you will be taken care of upon my death."

Baroness Von Duty tittered as she sat next to her husband. "Oh, my dear, of course I will be. You have so much money we will be taken care of for the rest of our lives."

Cinder shook his head again. Money was all it was ever about. *She'll be bitterly disappointed when she finds out she spent it all...*

CHAPTER TWO

Two days later, Cinderfella was called into his father's chambers. "Father, what is it, are you not long for this life?" He grasped his father's cold withered hand and sat beside him on the huge four-poster bed, his eyes searching his father's for answers.

The old man's breath rasped in and out. "Cinder… I am close to my end…but there is something I must tell you before I go…" He pointed to a small wooden box on his bedside cupboard. "It is for you…for your eighteenth birthday…no, no, do not open it…" He stopped Cinder from seeing its contents too early. "You must open it only in two days on your birthday."

"What is it, Father?" Cinder eyed the small carved box in his hands.

"It is from your mother," the man rasped. "A letter explaining everything, plus some bits and pieces. They are important…but only for your birthday." He patted his son's hand. "I am so proud of you and the man you have become, Cinderfella. Promise me you will keep it until your birthday." He looked at his doctor and lawyer who were also in the room. "You understand what I am doing?" They nodded. "Good. Now, fetch my wife, I must say my goodbyes."

The doctor spoke to a maid outside the door and she scurried away to find her mistress.

Baroness Von Duty came bursting into the room in a flurry of bright coloured taffeta and hoop skirts only moments later. "Darling, you cannot be leaving me." She flung herself onto the bed beside him. "It is not your time."

Cinderfella stood beside the doctor and lawyer, grasping his box. Out of the corner of his eye he noticed his stepbrothers sidle into the room and silently stand at the end of the bed.

They watched the scene with great interest until Wilhelm noticed the box in Cinder's hand. With a slight gesture, he got Mikhale's interest piqued too.

"Nooooo," the Baroness cried. "My husband is dead, dead, dead, he is dead."

Cinder moved forward with the doctor. "Father? Father?"

"Get away, get away from my husband," the Baroness hissed.

"He was *my* father before he was *your* husband!" Cinder's insult was like a slap in the face for the Baroness whose tears were immediately replaced with hatred. He glanced at the doctor. "Is he?"

The doctor nodded. "I'm sorry, Cinderfella, Baroness, but the Baron is dead."

Cinder gently touched his father's shoulder. "Goodbye, Father. You're better off now."

The Baroness' head twitched. "What do you mean…better off…*now*?"

"Exactly what I said," he snapped, stepping back to stand beside the lawyer. "What now?" He heard a whoosh of taffeta. "What happens now?"

"Yes, Mr Van Buren, what happens now?" The Baroness stood beside her stepson.

Mr Van Buren was nonplussed by the Baroness. "The doctor takes him to the morgue and a burial date will be set. The reading of the will will be in town in two days." He glanced at Cinder. "That is also your eighteenth birthday."

A small grim smile showed for a moment on Cinder's face. "Won't be much of a birthday though, will it?" He gently touched the box in his hand. "I guess this is all I have left, of not only my mother, but now my father."

The Baroness eyed the box and reached out to snatch it. *"Give it to me; that's mine."*

Van Buren's hand snaked out and caught her arm, making her jump in surprise. "No, Baroness." His tone stopped her short. "That is *not* yours. It belongs to Cinder. It's from his mother and so did not belong to the Baron. You have *no right* to it."

"But everything in this house belongs to me," she screeched. "It is all mine, every last piece is mine."

"That's where you're *wrong.*" Van Buren smoothly deflected her. "It isn't. Everything in this house is *not* yours." He watched her hateful expression deflate. "In fact, you'll be quite surprised in two days at just exactly *what is* yours." He turned to Cinder. "Why don't you leave? The doctor and I will take care of your father. We'll make sure everything works out properly." He laid a hand on Cinder's shoulder. "We'll see you in town in a couple of days."

Cinderfella nodded. "All right." He glanced at his stepmother. "Do you think you can resist stealing for the next two days?" He almost laughed at her shocked expression.

"*Me?*" Her eyes widened. "*Steal?* From *my own* house? From *my own* husband?" Her hand went to her mouth in shock. "I *cannot believe* you could say such a thing after all this time I've looked after you and your father."

"Ha! Looked after!?" he replied. "Is *that* what you call it?" He glanced at the sons. "I know for a fact that you two have been selling our goods in town." He turned from their shocked expressions back to the Baroness. "You just wanted my father's money. You never loved him and you sure as heck never cared about me." He stormed through the door and left the house.

*****

Two days later, on Cinderfella's eighteenth birthday, the will was to be read. Only a few people were bequeathed anything, so they gathered in the lawyer's office at ten o'clock.

Van Buren walked in. "Are we ready for the reading of the will?"

Cinder glanced at his stepmother and stepbrothers before his gaze went to Mr Shelton the stable manager, Mr Braddon the estate manager, and a few other people he did not know.

"This is the last will and testament of Baron Freddard Von Duty, the fifth Baron of East Etton. To my estate and stable managers, I bequeath one hundred pounds each. To Mr Shorten and Mr Brennen, I bequeath one hundred pounds each and all accounts paid."

Cinder glanced at the four men standing at the back of the room. *I wonder what accounts Father referred to. I check the accounts every week and don't remember seeing their names.* He turned back to the front.

"To my only son, Cinderfella, I bequeath everything else. He—"

"What?" the Baroness interrupted. "What do you mean *every*thing else?" Her eyes could have set a barn ablaze and her neck was going red. Leaning forward in her seat she slammed a hand on the desk. "*What do you mean…everything?* Do I get *nothing?* Why should lowly little Cinder get everything when I was his dutiful wife?" If looks could kill, the daggers she was sending Cinder's way would have killed him in seconds.

Cinder shifted in his seat. "What's going on, Van Buren?"

A sly smile slid across Van Buren's face. "Let me continue. To my only son, Cinderfella, I bequeath everything else. He becomes the sixth Baron of East

Etton, and so inherits the entire estate, the house and contents, the stable, the animals, the land. Everything I own, now belongs to my son."

"But-but-but," the Baroness sputtered. "What do *I* get? Does that mean *I am not Baroness anymore?*" She fluttered her delicate white lace handkerchief in front of her to get some air.

Van Buren continued, "To my *dear* wife and stepsons. Thank you for your care over the last two years. To the three of you, I leave a sum of one hundred pounds a year from the interest of the estate until Cinderfella turns twenty-one, at which time you get nothing. I know what you have taken from me, making sure to spend my money frivolously on trivial things. This is all you deserve. I will allow you to stay in the house for two days until the grand ball is over because I know you all have tickets, but in two days' time, you will be escorted out of the house. And *don't* think of stealing anything, there is a *very* detailed list of items, and your persons and your luggage will be checked before leaving."

Van Buren cleared his throat. "Now *that* is everything." His eyes went back and forth between Cinder and the Baroness, watching emotions flicker across their faces before resting on the men at the back of the room. "Gentlemen, my secretary has your money. Please sign the receipt on the way out." He waved a hand toward the door and watched them go.

The stepbrothers paled and sat heavily on a couch to the side of the room.

"But-but-but…" The Baroness' voice couldn't catch on another word as all words seemed to have left her. She spun in her seat to glare blatant black hatred at Cinderfella, who in turn eyeballed her with anger and shifted in his own seat.

"*You,*" her voice boomed. Her long delicate right forefinger rose to point at the boy she despised. "*You!*" Her voice slid to a hiss. "*You* did this. *You* made your father leave me out of the will. *You* somehow got in his ear and turned him against me." She stood in a rustle and swish of taffeta and moved two steps toward him. "*You did this to me—*"

"Actually," Van Buren interrupted, "the Baron wrote his will just over two years ago. Just before he *married* you, Baroness." He waited for the explosion.

It took a while to sink in, but finally the Baroness realised what he meant and gave him what he was waiting for. "*What?!*" exploded out of her. "*What do you mean he wrote it before we were married? He couldn't have? It couldn't be?*" She faltered and grabbed the chair for support. "He left me out of his will before he married me…"

Van Buren was enjoying seeing her get her comeuppance. He knew all about Madame Neila and her marriages. The Baron was husband number five, and he'd warned him before marrying her. The Baron had already heard the stories and heeded his lawyer's warnings, writing up a new will, leaving it all to Cinderfella, before proposing. Smart man, that Baron.

Cinder stood. "I will see to it that you get your

first one hundred pounds, Madame. You will need it to get to the ball and for accommodation and travel. Meanwhile," he bowed his head to the lawyer, "thank you, Mr Van Buren. I must go as I need to get ready for the ball myself."

Madame Neila turned on him as her sons laughed. "*You? Go to the ball?* Since when were *you* invited to the grand ball in the princess's honour?"

"Since *I* am the son of a Baron," he replied curtly, stopping their laughter in its tracks. "And since *I* was born on the same day as the princess. Every baby born on the same day eighteen years ago received an invitation way back then." He looked from Madame's face to his now ex-stepbrothers' jealousy. "You can hire a carriage in town before you go home. I'll be using the Von Duty carriage. After all," he added as he brushed some imaginary lint off his coat, "I am now the *sixth* Baron of East Etton." Placing his hat on his head, he added, "Good day and good riddance to you all." He walked out the door and headed home.

Once home, he instructed all of the servants to keep an eye on the Baroness for the next two days, and to the rest of the workers to watch out for the sons in case someone tried something sneaky. He hurriedly hooked up the family carriage in readiness for the ball, then went up to his room for supper and a bath.

"*You cannot do this to me, Cinderfella, you just can't. I own it all! It is all mine.*" Madame Neila stormed into Cinder's room and faced him in the bath. "I *do not care* for that will and it is *all a lie.* And as for you going to the ball, well, just look at you." She stopped pacing and waved her fan. "You're *a boy.* The princess would *not* be interested in you and besides, *you* have *nothing* to wear."

Cinder casually stood to face his stepmother whose eyes diverted in surprise when she saw the muscular adult body of her stepson. "My, Cinder…" She fanned herself quickly, averting her eyes and then glancing back.

"Yes, Madame Neila, *look* at me," he coolly replied. "I'm *hardly* a boy anymore." He casually grabbed a towel and wrapped it around his waist before stepping out of the bath. "My suit's brand new, and now that I'm the *sixth* Baron of East Etton, I can do whatever I like." He picked up some grapes from the supper tray and ate them. "And I ask *you*, Baroness, to leave my room so I can get ready for the ball." He waved his arm at the door. "Don't let it hit you on the hooped skirts on the way out."

With her gaze sliding up and down his masculine body, Madame Neila moved slowly for the door. "Are you seeing anyone special…Cinder?" Her lashes fluttered behind her fan as she walked into the hall.

"Get out, Baroness." He slammed and locked the door behind her.

Taking his time to dress, he thought back through the years when his mother told him about the ball. How he was automatically invited because he and the princess shared the same special day. How it was his lifelong duty to attend, and that he must *at all costs,* and how his eighteenth birthday was special for another reason. This reason he would find out only on the very day of his birthday.

His reminiscing reminded him of the box his father had given him, and after doing up his shirt buttons, he pulled the box from a hidey-hole in the floor under the bed. He sat down and looked at it.

Gently running his fingers over the intricately carved details, Cinder started remembering details about the box. It sat on his mother's desk under the window in the sitting room, basking in sunlight every afternoon. He always wondered what she kept in there, and finally, one day, he had a peek. It was just papers and stamps. He'd been so disappointed that there wasn't something more exciting hiding in there.

Lifting the lid, he once again saw papers and smiled. But these papers were a little different. One was a five page letter from his mother. He started reading and got to the third page. "Whoa…"

Meanwhile…

CHAPTER THREE

"Oh, Princess, your hair looks so pretty," the maid said as she finished the last curl.

Princess Charming's hair was delicate golden silk that shone in the sunlight. She sighed and propped her chin on her hand while leaning on her ginormous dressing table in her ginormous bedroom. "Yes, yes," she muttered. "You say that every time you do my hair, Dresdeldra." She gazed into the ginormous mirror, eyeballing the latest hairstyle her maid had given her. *Mmm, not bad.* Turning her head from side to side, Princess noticed the finely curled curls piled on top of her head and the wispy ones around her ears and neck.

Dresdeldra held out a tiara, but Princess waved it away. "Not yet. We'll put that on last." She got up from the table, wandered over to the double doors that led out to the balcony, and stood basking in the sun flowing down. "Another day, another ball." She sighed again, feeling that boring, bored out of her brains feeling she got whenever she attended another dreary gala held by her parents or friends of theirs.

"But this is *different,* Princess. It is your eighteenth birthday and the ball is in your honour." Dresdeldra stood beside her on the balcony. "At least the weather is good."

Princess smiled. "Yes, it is very good weather. How much longer till the ball? I'm starving. And I don't even know if I'll get to eat."

"About two more hours, I think—" Dresdeldra started before Princess flew from the room…

She flew down the long marble hall, down two ginormous marble staircases, along another marble hall, down a flight of wooden stairs, and into the ginormous stone floor basement kitchen.

"Oh, look at all that food." She hungrily eyed the cakes and jellies, and ducks and chickens roasted to perfection on the long table in the middle of the room. Her stomach growled and she dived for the closest chicken, managing to rip off a leg before being sprung.

"*Princess Charming* that is *no way* for a young lady to eat. And why can't you wait until the ball before stuffing your face?"

Princess had stopped dead with a mouthful of food, but now swallowed. "Because I'm hungry *now!*" she managed before sticking the rest of the leg in her mouth. She picked up another and grabbed a roasted potato. "Oh, God, so hungry."

"For goodness' sake, child," Mrs Button, the kitchen manager chastised. "At least sit down and I'll get you a plate. Have you not eaten today?" She laid an empty plate on the table and pushed aside others overflowing with rich goodies.

"Wasn't hungry till now," Princess mumbled around biscuits and thick chocolate cake. "But now I'm starving."

"Well slow down or you'll give yourself indigestion." Mrs Button started moving the food. "We must keep it chilled for tonight. God help us if you can't fit into your dress, or have no room for any birthday cake," she said as she walked out of the room with a huge platter of fruit.

"Berfday cay?" Princess perked up. "You meam I haf berfday cay?" She swallowed. "Is it here? Where, show me!"

Mrs Button came back for more dishes. "For goodness sake, considering you just inhaled enough food for two grown men I'm not about to let you *anywhere near* that cake, or there won't be any left for tonight."

"Aaaaarrrrhhhhh." The burp that came out of Princess was more that of a big adult man than a delicate eighteen-year-old young lady.

Mrs Button glared at her. "You'd better not be doing that tonight either."

Princess blushed and covered her mouth. "I'll try not to." Shovelling another biscuit into her mouth, she raced upstairs to the arts room, sliding to a halt when she spied the spears and staffs on the wall.

The arts room was a ginormous room for everything as it was so long there was a piano and painting easel at one end, and martial arts goodies at the other, with a whole bunch of things in between, like a ping pong table and mini croquet ground.

Princess picked up a staff and felt the weight of it in her hands before spinning it around in circles. With her eyes closed, she kept spinning the staff and slowly lifted her right leg. Putting her foot on her left knee, she balanced on one leg and spun the staff before spinning herself around to point the staff to the neck of her instructor. "Ha, yah!" She took the stance of a warrior. "I heard a noise. You know better than to sneak up on someone, Master Whan."

The medium built moustached Asian man stood tall with his hands clasped behind his back. "*Who* is sneaking, dear Princess? I was merely walking into the room."

She relaxed and lowered the staff. "How was I to know *that*, Master Whan?" She replaced the staff before continuing. "Are you here for the ball later?"

"Yes. Your parents have invited me. I could not miss one of my prize pupil's birthdays." He paused. "In fact; my other prize pupil will be here tonight celebrating a birthday as well. So I will see both of you tonight." With a small bow of his head he silently left the room.

Another prize pupil? Princess frowned. *I don't know if I like the fact I'm not the only one. I wonder who else he teaches.*

Lost in thought, she wandered back upstairs to her room. Its balcony overlooked the main driveway, so she would be able to see who was coming for the ball. *Maybe I'll be able to figure out who his other pupil is?*

"Oh, there you are, Princess." Dresdeldra was hanging five gorgeous dresses on a rack. "Here's your choice for tonight. Have you picked yet?"

"Mmm?" Princess lost her train of thought. "What?" She sat on the love seat at the end of the bed. "I didn't hear you."

Dresdeldra rolled her eyes. "Have you picked a dress yet?"

Looking over each one with a critical eye, Princess dismissed all but the turquoise blue silk and taffeta gown. "But I'll add the sashes from the deep rose one," she called out as the maid took the others back to the ginormous walk in closet, uh, make that ginormous room, full of Princess's things.

She had everything a princess would need, and everything a king and queen could buy for their precious only child. She had shoes, bags, hats, gowns, jewels and tiaras galore. Except she did not want any of them, or the castle, or money and fame; she wanted *more*. *More* adventure, *more* friends, *more* travel. But alas, her parents wanted to marry her off to some prince or earl or lord or something in the hope of producing an heir to the throne. They didn't understand Princess's thirst for adventure and knowledge, and wished she were more like the other young ladies her age who did needlepoint and had tea and scones in the afternoon. But she wasn't like them and refused to conform, instead taking up archery, martial arts, horse riding and swimming.

"Time to get ready, guests will be arriving soon."

Dresdeldra came back with the rose sashes and picked up the turquoise gown. She helped Princess into it and tied the sashes around her teeny tiny waist and her golden hair.

Princess topped off the gown with matching dancing slippers and her sapphire tiara. "There." She plonked it on her head. "I'm done. Let's see who's arriving."

Meanwhile...

CHAPTER FOUR

Cinderfella walked down the stairs to find Madame Neila and her sons waiting for their carriage. "Enjoy yourselves tonight, won't you." He straightened a cuff. "Since it will be the last ball you attend for a while."

"Cinder," Madame soothed. "Would you be so kind as to let us stay longer, at least until we have accommodation?" She fluttered her extra-long lashes behind her fan. She was dressed in a low-cut scarlet coloured velvet gown; her sons wore matching sashes with their suits. "You're still so young and in need of a…" she blinked slowly, "…*womanly* influence." She glanced away shyly. "We don't want you being taken advantage of…now do we…?"

Cinder knew that look. It was the look of a woman out for whatever she could gain. And *he* was it. "Like you haven't already? You've *already* taken advantage of my father, and now you're trying it on with me." Her expression turned spiteful. "I may be *young*, Madame, but I *am not* stupid." He leaned in to her. "I know a con woman when I see one. Now," he said as he tilted his head, "I do believe your carriage has arrived." Opening the door he waved them through. "Don't stay out too late," he called. "We don't want your carriage turning into a pumpkin or something at midnight, now do we?"

He watched them leave the estate before his own carriage pulled up. "Masters." He nodded to the driver while patting Steed, his favourite stallion on the nose. "Hey, old boy," he whispered. "*We're* off to the ball."

Meanwhile…

Princess was standing by her window, discreetly hidden by the curtains, watching the parade of buggies and carriages. "Ugh, too old, too fat, too bald. Goodness, Dresdeldra, I barely know these people. They must only be here for the celebrations and free food."

The maid stood beside her. "It is your eighteenth, something to celebrate, so of course your parents would show you off to everyone they know."

"Which is practically the whole kingdom and then some." Princess peered at a carriage. "Oh, my, they *cannot* be the sons of the King and Queen of Lancaster?" She watched two strapping young men descend from the carriage followed by their parents. "Good heavens, they've grown."

"Into fine young men," Dresdeldra murmured from her side.

They watched another carriage come to a stop and

a woman in scarlet velvet alight with two young men.

"Meh." Princess stepped back. *"So. not. hot."*

"Princess."

She turned. "Mummy, Daddy." She ran over and kissed them on both cheeks.

"Darling, we wanted to wish you happy birthday in private before going downstairs." The king was resplendent in his regalia and velvet cape. The crown upon his head was the biggest in all the land. He'd made sure of it.

That is why he also suffers headaches, Princess thought, *but silly Daddy doesn't think the pain is from the weight of the crown.* "Thank you, Daddy." Princess stood patiently. "But you really *didn't* need to do all of this. I'm *only* eighteen." Turning to her mother she took her hand. "Seriously, Mummy, what will you do when I'm twenty-one?"

Queen Charming laughed. It was light and dainty like her and suited her delicate pale pink dress and small gold tiara.

"We'll have an *even bigger* ball," the king boomed and beckoned to Dresdeldra. "Please leave us alone, we want a word with our daughter."

She curtsied and left the room.

"Mummy? Daddy?" She looked from one to the other. "This isn't another *'it's time for you to marry'* speech is it?" She spun around and huffed over to her ginormous bed where she flopped down amidst an array of turquoise material. "Because I'm *not* interested."

King and Queen Charming exchanged a look

and reached out for each other's hand. "No, dear," the king said. "This is something we must tell you tonight, and it's imperative that we do since it's your birthday."

Princess crossed her arms in a huff. "What does my birthday have to do with anything? I'm bored, can't we just go downstairs?"

"Princess," the king started before glancing at his wife.

Their daughter noticed the exchange. "Oh, for goodness' sake, just tell me."

The king started again and told Princess such a terrific tale she could say only one word as her eyes went wide.

"Whoa…"

Meanwhile…

Cinderfella eyed the mega sized castle as his carriage approached the circular driveway out front. *Well,* he thought. *This is impressive. But of all nights to be here…*

A footman opened his door and he alighted. Straightening his sash and suit, he slowly ascended the grand marble staircase to the main doors that were wide open for the party.

He paused in the doorway, searching the room for people he knew, but except for Madame and her sons, he knew no one.

Making his way slowly round the room, he made sure to avoid ex-relatives so there were no confrontations.

He accepted a glass of punch from a maid, and kept on walking out the back of the room into the garden. Standing amongst the flowers and shrubs, he took in the sweet summer scents of the evening.

Meanwhile...

"Whoa," Princess repeated, her mind a jumble of everything they had just told her. She was definitely having a hard time believing it. Walking around the room in a daze, she tried to put her thoughts together. "But I... But you... But how..." She turned to her parents. "I, when, how?"

"We know this is something that will be overwhelming and maybe..." Queen Charming walked over to her daughter and grasped her hand. "This is something we could have told you this morning instead of waiting until right before your party. But..." she paused to look at her husband and added, "It doesn't matter, you needed to be told today. That's all, before the party."

"Because..." The king paused this time. "They may be here at the party...tonight."

"Why would they be *here?*" Princess shook her head, looking back and forth at them, wanting more answers than she was being given. "Why tonight? What do they want?"

The monarchs exchanged another nervous glance. "They...want...*you,* dear."

The knock at the door interrupted the moment and a butler stuck his head in. "Your guests are waiting, Your Majesty."

"Thank you, Reginald," the king replied. "Darling, look…" He waited for the door to close. "As long as you were told today, and you stay on guard, no harm should come to you. You've been doing martial arts for eight years now, you're very good, and Master Whan is here to help if needed."

She frowned. "*That's* why you invited him? So that he could help. Help with what?"

"Help with saving you in case they come to take you, or do harm," her father replied. "Look, I know this is a lot, but let's freshen up and get downstairs. Just keep an eye out for any shady looking people."

Yes, Princess thought, *because I really know what shady looking people look like…*

Meanwhile…

CHAPTER FIVE

"Your Majesties, Kings, Queens, Lords and Ladies, Barons and Baronesses, Counts and Countesses, etc, Ladies and Gentlemen, lowly peasants… Will you please take your place in line to wish Princess Charming a happy birthday."

Cinderfella reluctantly meandered over to the side of the room to line up. He didn't want to spend hours waiting in line just to say happy birthday to some snobby spoilt brat. He looked at the line behind him then turned around. He was about one third in and noticed his ex-stepmother had managed to get in just ahead of him.

Ugh, boring! He inwardly sighed and tried not to make small talk with those around him. Balls were just not his thing; of course they weren't since he'd never attended one. He pulled at his collar and scratched underneath. *Ugh, itchy. Why was I even invited to this thing? It's my birthday too, and I could be spending it how I want instead of waiting for some rich kid to show up to the big party her parents have thrown just to show the county how rich they are. She probably looks like a pig in mud.*

"Your Majesties, Madams, Monsieurs, Ladies and Gentlemen, pig farmers and stable boys, etc… may I announce the princess, Princess Charming."

Cinder looked around for a girl before realising the royal family was descending the stairs just ahead of him to his right.

He gasped. He gaped.

He stared at the golden wonder wrapped in turquoise that was Princess Charming; a girl as beautiful as any rose he'd ever seen.

She gracefully descended the stairs with her parents behind her.

He stopped.

At least she has parents!

His mood deepened and he slipped into glumness; a glumness that was still there an hour later as he approached her on her dais.

"Baroness Von Duty and her sons, Mikhale and Wilhelm."

"Hello, how do you do, thank you so much for coming," Princess graciously said.

"Oh, Princess, it's such an honour to have been invited." The Baroness exuded such sickeningly sweet, fake rubbish that Cinder thought he was going to be sick.

Baroness, he silently harrumphed. *Not anymore!*

"Let me introduce my son, Mikhale." She shoved him toward the dais.

"Princess." He willingly kissed the hand she extended.

"Thank you for coming." She carefully extricated her hand from his while keeping a smile on her delicate face and her composure in check.

"And Wilhelm." Her other son was pushed forward and he shoved his brother aside.

"Princess," he said, his voice as smooth as a baby's bottom. "Your beauty has captured my eyes, and your voice, my heart. So lovely to meet you." He took her hand and pulled her toward him, trying to lay a kiss on her lips.

"Oh, oh," she cried, "get off me."

Master Whan silently stepped forward and removed Wilhelm from the princess' way.

"I'm so sorry," the Baroness said, swatting at her son with her fan. "I'm so sorry, Princess. I *did not* raise him to be like that." Footmen scurried forward and hurried Madame and her sons away. Princess straightened her dress and stood back on her podium.

Cinderfella watched in great horror at the scene. *They have the gall to disgrace my father's name?* he simmered. *How dare they after everything they've done.* He moved forward in the line and his attention moved to his martial arts instructor. *I wonder why Master Whan is here. He certainly moved quickly to deactivate the situation.*

"The sixth Baron of East Etton, Baron Cinderfella Von Duty."

Still in a bad mood, he swung his head around to gaze at the golden goddess before him, standing there shining like a rose in the sunlight. His mood didn't change.

She looked puzzled. "Von Duty?" She pointed to the Baroness and her sons on the far side of the room.

"Ex-stepmother," he replied coolly. "Disgracing my father's name and reputation, giving it a good tarnishing, sadly. He died only two days ago, and here I am on *my* birthday attending *your* birthday party."

She stood there shocked, for no one had ever spoken to her in such a disinterested, cool manner before.

Cinder glanced at her parents. "At least you *have* parents for your birthday."

"Oh." Her eyes went wide. "I-I'm so sorry about your father." She clasped her hands in front of her, willing them to stop from shaking. *How dare he speak to me that way?* She wanted to knock his block off.

"Yeah." Cinder sniffed. "Thanks, nice meeting you." He wandered off to the right and into another room.

"What a rude young man," the king muttered.

Princess spun around. "Did you not just hear him, Father? He lost his father two days ago and today is *his* birthday too. He's hardly in the mood to celebrate." She turned back to her guests and continued the greetings.

"Well, Cinderfella, look at you," Mikhale muttered as he and his brother wandered into the room where he was.

"What do you two want?" He took a deep breath

and willed his feet to move toward the door for he had wanted privacy and silence, not chaos and mayhem.

"Why are *you* here, Cinderfella?" Wilhelm asked. "Princess Charming is *too* good for you. You just proved it by shunning her, at *her* party, on *her* birthday."

Cinder rolled his eyes. "And you two *are* good enough for her? That's a joke. I'm here because I'm the *sixth* Baron of East Etton, Baron Von Duty, and since you two don't have a royal or noble title, why are *you* here?" He watched their smug faces turn green with envy.

Mikhale sneered. "We may not have a fancy title like you, but we have a very important reason for being here, Cinder...*fella*."

"Mikhale," Wilhelm warned sharply. "Let's leave Cinder to his misery. After all, he no longer has parents." They burst out laughing and left the room.

"But at least I have an estate and money," he called after them. *Ugh! Thank God they're out of my life.*

Out of the darkness came, "Your Majesties, Your Royal Highnesses, Madams and Monsieurs, Ladies and Gentlemen and everybody else who shouldn't be here...we will now have the royal dance, where every eligible male *and* boy under twenty-five will dance with Princess Charming."

"Ugh," Cinderfella repeated, glancing around his dark cocoon. *Maybe I could just slip out the door unnoticed and go home.*

"Cinderfella."

He turned to see Master Whan and bowed. "Master, I noticed that you were here. I'm surprised that you would come to an eighteenth birthday party."

The martial artist glided over. "I am here for something much more important and so are you, Cinderfella. There may come a time tonight when you will have to defend Princess Charming against evil. Evil is very strong tonight."

Cinder felt like rolling his eyes. "Evil? Does that *actually* exist?"

The Asian narrowed his eyes. "Yes, Cinder, it does. Remember everything I taught you, and use it to the best of your ability. Now, go out there and dance with Princess."

"But I—"

"*Dance!*"

Having always been wary of Master Whan's sharp tone, Cinder's uneasy feelings got worse as he dragged his feet through the door and into the grand ballroom. *What is going on? And why does Master Whan think evil is afoot?*

He was jostled toward the centre of the room where he saw Mikhale dancing with Princess. *He's not twenty-five; they must both be at least thirty.*

He was announced. "Baron Von Duty."

Pushed into the space, he came face to face with Mikhale, who looked so angry he might've punched Cinder in the face if it weren't for the presence of Princess. "It is still my turn," he hissed in a low tone so she did not hear him.

Cinder wasn't fazed. "You know, you hiss just like your mother." He noticed her off to the side with anger all over her face. "Time to go, Mikhale, the princess is bored with your attention." He pushed him aside and put his hands up for the princess to take. Dutifully, stiffly, they danced around the room.

"I'm terribly sorry about your father." She tried small talk. "That must have been horrible to lose him two days before your birthday."

He glanced at the faces around them, a welcome distraction from the rays of light emitting from her big blue eyes. "Yes, yes it was."

"So…" She was busy noticing his muscular physique. "I should wish *you* a happy birthday too then." She wondered if he was into sports and then opened her mouth again. "What sort of a name is Cinderfella for a boy?" *Ugh, why did I have to say that?*

He glanced down, a frown on his face. "*You're* asking *me? Your* parents named you Princess, so don't get all judgy."

She blushed a little and rolled her eyes. "Yeah, I know, great name huh? The princess, Princess Charming. It's horrible being announced at balls and galas."

"Because we *all* have to worry about being announced at balls and galas. Talk about first world problems." Cinder's sarcasm made her blush again. "Well," he added, "they *could* have done better if they had tried." He eyed her beet red face and big blue eyes, making her blush harder. The song ended and they came to a twirling stop without breaking from each other. He stared down at the dainty girl in his arms.

"Um," she mumbled, not sure where to look or how to control the racing heartbeat in her chest. "Since it's your birthday too…we could share my cake."

That scored a small grin from him. "Is it any good?"

She grinned in reply. "It's chocolate!"

His lips slid up into a smile, the first he'd had in many days. "My favourite."

"And now the next dance…"

Another young man came over and Cinder reluctantly let go.

"I'll see you later, at the cake," she called as she was swept away.

CHAPTER SIX

An hour later, she stood in front of a huge ten layer cake that was twice as tall as she was, in the shape of a castle, obviously, and towering above her. After having a very loud and rowdy happy birthday sung to her, she eagerly sliced into one of the middle layers to reveal a decadent triple chocolate layer cake. After cutting two slices, she handed over the knife to the butler and proceeded over to Cinder. "Here's your cake." The plate she held had a ginormous piece on it.

"That is *way* too much for one person." He took the plate and fork. "I don't think I'll be able to get through it." He tasted a bit. "Mmm, good."

Princess inhaled half of her slice. "Well, if you can't finish yours, I'll have it." She inhaled the rest while he looked on in disbelief with his fork perched mid-air.

"Do you…" he hesitated, "…normally…eat like that?"

She blinked slowly…innocently… "Like what?"

He stared into those big blue innocent eyes. "Like a vacuum cleaner?"

"Oh." She blushed and wiped her mouth with her napkin. "Yep."

A grin slowly slid across his face. "I like a woman who isn't scared of food and knows how to eat." He continued gazing at her exquisite beauty.

She perked up. "Interesting."

"What?"

"I like a man who likes a woman who isn't scared of food and knows how to eat."

It was Cinder's turn to blush, which was unusual as men didn't blush, especially him, and especially because of what a woman had said. And on top of that, women, or young ladies, had never spoken to him like that anyway. The kind of way that made him blush.

"Baron." King and Queen Charming came over. The king's expression was not pleasant. "You're the young man who was rude to my daughter before."

Cinder stood his ground, and with a tilt of his head he agreed. "I was, and I must apologise. It hasn't been a good few days for me."

The king nodded. "Yes, yes, your father, Baron Von Duty. I met him a few times a few years ago. I had some dealings with him and bought some horses. Fine horses they were too, and still are. Good man, your father."

"Thank you, sir." Cinder was warmed at the mention of his father. "I trained the horses you bought. My father spoke highly of you."

"You trained them, hey." The king scratched his chin. "Then you're very good at whatever it is you do. Fine horses. Fine, fine, horses."

"Darling, let's leave Princess to her guest. Remember dear," said the queen as she touched Princess on the arm. "Keep an eye out." They wandered off, casting curious glances back over their shoulders to the young man that had caught their daughter's eye.

Her last sentence intrigued him. "An eye out for what? My sleazy ex-stepbrothers?"

Princess giggled. "And any like them. Shall we take a walk in the garden?"

He shrugged. "Why not."

They wafted through the room and out onto the terrace, and drifting down the stairs, they stopped to admire the scents emitting from the flowers.

Cinder was lost in thought.

"Hello, anyone there, hello?"

"What?" He came to.

"I said..." Princess clearly didn't like being ignored, but she might forgive it for this one young man who had so captured her attention. "It's not much of a birthday for you then?"

"No." Cinder gently touched a rose. "The first one without both parents."

"I'm sorry. When did your..."

"When I was twelve."

"So then, when did your father marry the evil stepmother?"

"Two years ago."

They stopped beside a huge round pool and sat on the side.

"That must have been hard. Your mother, the stepmother, and then your father." She wanted to learn more about him and was very nearly drowning in the depths of his eyes.

Cinder grinned. "It was, but when we found out my father left her only three hundred pounds in his will, it made it easier."

"Why so little? Do you not have money? You're a baron after all?" She leaned toward him, curious and hanging on every word.

He gazed into her delicate face, unsure of how much to tell her. After all, he didn't know her from a bar of soap, so why should he tell her anything? But she was...delicate and...*charming...* "We did. She spent a lot of it in the last two years, but Father was smart." His grin got bigger. "And so was I. We kept a lot of it from her. I may not have what you do..." He swept his eyes over the palatial castle and grounds. "But I'm happy with what I have."

There was a rustling of a nearby bush and they turned in its direction.

"Who's there? Come out and show yourself." Cinder stood to confront whoever was eavesdropping. "Be a man and show yourself."

"Cinder," Princess urged with a hand on his arm. "Go and check it out."

"Will you be all right here?" he asked, lightly touching her hand.

"Yes, go."

Cinder ran to the bush and dived in, preparing to tackle the person head on.

"Aaaahhhhhhh…"

Hearing the scream, he landed awkwardly, and realised there was actually no one there. "Princess?" He pulled himself up and raced back to the spot he'd left her, only for her to be gone…

CHAPTER SEVEN

"Take your filthy hands off me," Princess spat, slapping away the dirty hands of Mikhale and Wilhelm. "Who do you think you are, grabbing me like that? And how did you get me here? Was that a puff of smoke?" She looked around. "Where are we? Where have you taken me? How did we get here?"

Madame Neila approached her. "Calm down, Princess. We aren't going to hurt you...yet!"

"What do you mean...yet?" Princess snapped, brushing off her dress. "Look at my dress, it's dirty, you've ruined it. I'll make you pay for this. Daddy will *not* be happy. I want to go home *now*." She turned around, but saw only forest. "Where *are* we?"

"Somewhere no one will find us while we do our work."

"What? What are you talking about?"

"Oh, for goodness' sake stop talking! Mikhale, gag her." Madame Neila walked toward a pile of rocks while Mikhale grabbed Princess and stuck a rag in her mouth.

She spat it out. "Pleh, pleh, pleh, don't you dare

touch me, and don't you dare stick some horrible gross rag in my mouth."

"That was a ten pound handkerchief," Mikhale complained. "*Not* a rag."

"I don't care *what* it was; keep it out of my mouth." Princess kicked him and stormed to the stone pile where Madame had lit candles. "What *are* you doing?"

The woman sighed. "Wilhelm, tie her up and gag her since your brother can't seem to do the job on his own."

"Mother," Mikhale protested, tucking the handkerchief into his pocket.

"Face it, Mikey, you're useless when it comes to women," Wilhelm teased, grabbing Princess by the arm. "Let me tie you up, like a *real* man would."

"Ow, don't touch me. Real man, huh." Princess picked up her dress. "Let's see if a real man can deal with this." She managed to wrench out of his grasp and perform a couple of high kicks in his face, knocking him backward so he landed with a thud on his butt.

"Mikhale, grab her," his mother cried.

Princess did a swing kick, a spin kick, and then flattened him out next to his brother. "Come on, ex-Baroness Von Duty." She danced around like a fighter, putting her fists up, ready to fight. "Come on and give it to me—"

Ding…dong…ding…dong…

Princess stopped and cocked her head. "Oh, my god, we're not that far from home."

"No, no," shouted Madame Neila. "Mikhale, Wilhelm, get up and help me, quickly." She placed trinkets around the stone pile and pulled out a small book. "Get up, you imbeciles."

Princess was disgusted. "That's no way to speak to your sons."

The boys struggled to their feet and made it to their mother's side before the bell struck twelve. "No," she shouted. "No."

With a burst of light brighter than a fireball, Madame Neila and her sons started changing. Their skin changed colour and sagged and stretched. Their bodies bent over, their hair fell out, their hands became crippled, and they grew old and ugly. The light subsided and all that was left was three decrepit old people.

Princess blinked slowly…and again…and a third time. "What…just…happened?" She was transfixed by what she had witnessed, the possibility of it being all too real.

"Midnight happened," cackled the person formerly known as Mikhale.

"We can still fix this," cried Madame Neila. "We just need her blood." She started chanting something from the book. "Weema woomoo weema woo."

"Oh, for goodness' sake." Princess crossed her arms. "*I'm* going home." She turned and stomped off in the general direction of the bell, but suddenly found herself floating in the air. "What the…?" She flew backwards until she landed in front of the stone pile, where Madame and her sons were waiting.

"You are not going anywhere until we get your blood, Princess Charming. And even then you will not live to tell the tale." Madame cackled. "I'll hold her down, Mikhale, you get your knife and drain her blood."

"Drain my?" Princess struggled to move. "What do you mean, *drain my blood?* Wait...are you the freaks my parents warned me about? The ones who might try to do something to me tonight." She spied the huge knife Mikhale produced and shivered. But what scared her more was the long green tongue that slid out from between his lips...

Cinderfella heard the scream across the field and took off running. He'd been searching for Princess, but came to the conclusion she'd gone back inside. Now, screams were echoing across the field, emanating from the forest in front of him.

He smashed through the underbrush, following the screams until he came upon the altar and three decrepit old people. One of them had a long green tongue that was licking Princess's bare neck and chest.

"Aaaaaahhhhhhhhh..."

"Princess, I'm here." He ran for her, not sure of what to do.

"Cinderfella, I'm so glad you're here." She nodded toward the old people. "They're attacking me and want my blood. Kill them."

"Stay back, Cinder, or I will kill you too. We need her blood. We will be done when Mikhale can get it."

"Mikhale?" Cinder paused, confused by the turn of events. He shook his head. "Wait, that can't be?"

"It is, it is," Princess cried. "They changed when the clock struck twelve."

"No, what do you mean they changed?" He was dazed, barely understanding what was going on, even though it was going on in front of him.

Madame Neila shook her head. "You stupid boy. We're witches, and we are here to take Princess's blood. You will not stop us."

"Witches?" Cinder remembered snatches of the letter he'd read. The letter from his mother. "*You're* witches?" he asked the person formerly known as his stepmother. "*All* of you? *Witches*?"

Wilhelm cackled. "You always were stupid, Cinder. You never got what we actually *were*, or *did*, for a living."

"Thieves," Cinder cried. "That's what you are. You spent my father's money and tried selling his belongings in town. Lowlife thieving crooks." He carefully glanced around to see if there was something for him to use.

"No, you need to stay out of it, Cinder. It is Princess's birthright. A promise was made eighteen years ago and I am here to collect." Neila went back to her spells. "She belongs to us, regardless of what you might do."

"Are you referring to the deal you made with my parents?" Princess piped up. "The one they made with a witch, so they could get a baby they so desperately wanted?" She struggled, but magic was holding her.

"A deal?" Cinder asked.

"Apparently," Princess replied. "My parents desperately wanted a baby, so they did a deal with a witch to get one. It was me, and now they told me that tonight the witch might pop up and try to take what she's owed."

"Which is?"

"My blood." Princess looked over at Madame Neila. "Is it *just* my blood?"

"Oh, for goodness' sake, both of you shut up," she snapped.

Cinder made his move. Doing a double roll over to the tree branch he had spied, he swung it at Madame Neila.

Ah," she cried, falling over, taking the candles with her and setting alight the grass around her.

"Mother!" Mikhale and Wilhelm let go of Princess and ran for their mother. Cinder ran for Princess who fell to the ground after the magic spell was broken.

"A deal with witches, huh?" he muttered. "Well, it's a good thing I found out today that I'm from a long line of witch hunters."

"Witch hunters," Princess whispered. "How did you find—"

"The letter my mother left me. I found out today."

"I will get you, Cinderfella Von Duty," Wilhelm cried out, stumbling to his feet.

"Do you know how to fight?" Cinder asked Princess.

"Master Whan is my sensei."

He was shocked. "He's mine too. Ah..." The breath left his body as he was lifted from the ground. Wilhelm held his arm out, his magic grasping Cinder by the throat.

"No," Princess cried, finding one of the rocks from the pile. She threw it with all her might and hit Wilhelm on the head. The broken magic let go of Cinder who fell to the ground.

He gasped for air. "Time to fight."

With the martial arts prowess Master Whan had taught them, they cartwheeled, rolled, and kicked their way to Madame Neila and her sons who tried to fight with their magic, but with ancestry of Cinder's witch hunting, they were no match, as Cinder grew stronger with every kick and punch.

Princess held her own. After slicing off her dress, she kicked the crap out of Mikhale and then Wilhelm, kicking and punching them back and forth between her and Cinder.

"Argh."

"Oomph."

"My sons..."

Cinder and Princess stopped and puffed for air. "Apparently there's only a few ways to kill witches," Cinder told them. "So prepare to die."

"Cinder, no, for the sake of your father." Madame Neila reached up to him with her old decrepit hand from her position on the ground. "Think of your father."

"My father," he spat. "He knew better...than to trust you. He knew who my mother was and the power she possessed. And now, I'd say he'd be glad I'm doing this." With a spin kick he knocked her flat.

"Argh."

He and Princess laid their groaning old bodies side by side.

"How many ways can you kill a witch?" Princess asked him, standing over them with her hands on her hips.

He took deep breaths until his breathing was back to normal. "There are three ways apparently, burn at the stake, knife to the heart, or chopping their heads off."

Princess delicately shuddered, a hand going to her neck. "Gory!"

"It is, but we must do all three to make sure they never do this again."

She stood back and crossed her arms, waiting for the finale. "Well, they're *your* family, you can do it then."

"Gee, thanks." Cinder picked up the knife. "For my father," he muttered.

CHAPTER EIGHT

After dealing with the bodies, they headed back to the castle.

"So, your birthday is over," Cinderfella said. "What will you do now?" He wiped his hands on the remnants of Princess's gown.

She sighed. "I don't know. My parents expected me to meet Prince Charming tonight and marry and have kids." She twirled around. "But I want to see the world, and travel to places far and wide, and meet lots of people. Hey," she stopped. "Your birthday's over too."

He grimaced. "Yeah, not much of a birthday. I find out I inherited my father's title and entire estate, and that his ex-wife and her sons were witches who were hell bent on fulfilling a promise made eighteen years ago. What a day."

"So, what do you plan on doing now?" She executed another twirl.

"According to my mother's letter, I'm descended from a long line of witch hunters. I didn't even know they existed until today."

"Yeah," she agreed. "Me neither. But I don't have to worry about dying now, so I'm footloose and fancy-free."

Cinder glanced at her twirling and skipping away on her shapely legs. "Seeing as we're both students of Master Whan, I might put that to good use by going into the witch hunting business." He'd been joking when he said it, but now that he thought about it, this seemed to make sense. And it felt right, as if he would be continually getting justice for his parents with every kill he made.

Princess stopped in front of him and clapped her hands in excitement. "Ohhh, witch hunting. Take me, take me, please, please, please," she begged, running around him like an excited puppy dog as he continued walking.

"Take you? Why would I take you? You're a *Charming*, I'd expect you to make your own way. *And* pay for it."

"Wait, what?" She raced after him. "Does that mean I can come? We'll travel the world together and fight evil witches here and abroad. We'll set up a business. A witch hunting business."

He laughed at her exuberance. "As long as you pay your own way, looks like we will."

"Well." She took his hand as they walked along. "We'll have to get some promotional stuff like banners or pamphlets and business cards made up. I can just see the tag line now. *'Cinderfella and Princess Charming: Witch Hunters'.*"

WWW.BADLUCK-
YOUREDEAD.COM

CHAPTER ONE

"Oh, my God." Mike charged up to me in the school rec room and slammed his books onto the table. "Have you seen that new website everyone on social media is talking about?" He sat down and slumped in the chair. "It's awesome, and I was up till early this morning checking it out."

I looked up from my assignment. "What website? I was actually doing homework last night—"

"And the night before and the night before," Mike cut in, pulling papers from a folder. "You never have any fun, Jordy. You need to cut loose sometimes and actually get on social media—"

"I have a life." I finished off a paragraph on sperm whales.

"Bahahahaha." Mike lolled around in his seat. "No, you don't. You're probably the only kid in year ten at Free Ridge High that doesn't have a life, and doesn't have any social media pages." He looked at me in all seriousness. "Dude, we *have* to get you online."

My head turned in his direction. "I *do* have a

life, and no, I don't need to *get* online." I shuffled a few papers looking for the notes I needed. "There are *way* too many problems with the kids at this school and what they're putting online and all the hassles they get from each other and all the hassles they get into. I'm *not* interested in that garbage."

"But you *might* be interested in *this*." Mike pulled a pen from his case, and after sorting his own papers and ripping the corner off one of them, he scribbled something down and handed it to me.

"www.badluck-youredead.com." I fingered the paper as I read it. "What's this supposed to be about?" It sounded as bad as it looked. Even on paper.

"Oh." Mike sat up and grabbed my arm. "It's the *coolest* thing. I was looking at every page and googling for details about it, but there wasn't much there. You can upload videos of people dying in horrific ways and stuff, and you can have chats with other users and ask about the videos." He leaned in and lowered his voice. "There's even a page where you can add the name of a person that you want to die." He looked furtively around the room making sure no one else heard him.

I stared at him, absolutely dumbfounded. "You're kidding?"

He stared back in amusement. "Isn't it awesome!"

*****

For the rest of the day all I heard was how awesome

this badluck-youredead site was. In the hallways, whisperings in class, at lunchtime, even on the bus home when all the kids sat transfixed staring at videos on the website. I shook my head in disgust. What is so much fun about watching videos of people dying? At home I watched the news with my parents before finishing off my assignment. I would rather educate myself on the ways of the world than watch horrific stuff like that.

*****

The next morning on the bus there were quiet whisperings and horrified expressions on my classmates' faces. I didn't know why until the Principal called an assembly.

"Everyone, please be silent." His voice boomed through the enormous confines of the school gym. His hand claps for our attention were short and sharp. We all quietened down.

"I have been informed that one of our students, a year eleven girl by the name of Maybelle Ryder, died sometime during the night."

Soft gasps and murmurs went through five thousand school kids and I sat stunned by the news.

"We have been told there is a video of her death on a particular website which we find quite horrifying." He ran his hand over his face and I got the feeling he'd seen it. He waved his hands towards the teachers standing off to the side. "There will be no classes today. We will take the day to talk to you, help you with any questions you'll have. We hope this will help you through the grieving process."

I looked over each teacher, noting postures and facial expressions. Sadness, shock, disbelief. The same expressions I saw on the faces of the students.

"We also have the police coming around to talk to you as a class and then individually. Mainly, they'll talk to Maybelle's friends and those who saw her last." He raised his hands at the confused mutterings from the students. "There's nothing to worry about. No one's being arrested. They just want information, and whatever you can tell them may help catch her killer. So please, I beg you, if you know something then please, tell them. Regardless of how insignificant you might think it is."

I saw uniformed officers pour through the door.

"Everyone dismissed."

"Whoa, dude. Can you believe that?" Mike rushed over as I walked down the hall to my classroom.

"Believe what?" I hefted my schoolbag onto my shoulder. "That someone from this school has died?" I stopped walking and faced him. "People die all the time, young and old, for whatever reason. We all die, Mike."

His brows flew up. "Dude, okay." He put his hands up in surrender. "No need to be so *adult* about it. I was talking about the fact that Maybelle's name was on the youredead death list, and now someone posted a video of her dying in the middle of the night."

We continued into our room and sat at our desks

before he continued. "Dude, someone *killed her* last night. *After* she was named. And *then* posted the video on the site." He shook his head in bewilderment. "I don't know whether that's freaky shit, or awesome."

"How about horrible and awful?" Janelle sat beside him at her desk.

I remembered she knew Maybelle through choir or something. "Guess the police will want to talk to you?" I said.

She glared at me. "And why do you say *that,* Jordan Belmont? Do you think *I* did it?" She angrily flipped her long thick hair over her shoulder. "Because *if that's* what you're saying…?"

"I said no such thing, actually." My smart reply made her stop. "But since you're both in choir, and choir practice was *last night* after school, you would have all been, potentially, the last ones to see her alive."

"Dude!" Mike piped up. "Have you memorised the entire school schedule or something?"

I smirked a little. "Yes, actually, I have."

Janelle had been thinking during our banter. "You're right, Jordan. We did and we were." A panicked look came over her face. "Oh, my God. What if the police think it's *me*?"

We all turned to the front as Mrs Mendoza walked into the room followed by a male and a female police officer. "Class," she called and clapped her hands to hush the excited murmur. "These officers would like to know if any of you saw Maybelle last night."

Mike and I pointed at Janelle who flashed us a furious glance in return.

"Janelle, dear, please follow these officers outside, you may be able to help."

CHAPTER TWO

"Dude, you have *got to watch* this video." Mike sat down beside me at our lunch table with his phone in hand. "It's awesome and gruesome and guess what?" He briefly looked up. "There's pictures of her dead body all over the internet, over *every* social media site…just…everywhere." He glued his eyes back to the screen. "I can't stop watching this."

"And *that* is why I'm not on social media," I replied dryly. "I told you the other day there's too much stuff on there, and kids here at school are too horrible to each other on it." I picked up my soda. "*Why* would I want to be a part of that?" Mike didn't flinch. "I'm serious. Tell me *why* I would want to be a part of that, because it causes nothing but grief."

Mike finally looked up. "Because it's *awesome*, dude. You're such a goody two shoes, Jordy. You're never late for school, or football practice. You have your assignments in before everyone else, *and* you have the school's curricular activities memorised. You *really* need to get a life, dude."

"Do you call everyone dude?" I smirked. "Or is it just reserved for me?"

"Nope! I call everyone dude, dude." He grinned and held up his phone. "Really, you *have* to see this."

I started to protest and push his hand away.

He pushed back. "Even if it's just for the sake of knowing what's going on in the school."

I sighed. God how I hated social media!

"Who knows," Mike cajoled. "You might even get an assignment out of it."

My ears pricked up at the word assignment. Thanks to my parents pushing me to get better grades and educate myself in the ways of the world, watching the news together every night and then having discussions about it, I always had great topics for my school assignments. I often got top marks and awards for my educated effort and ability to lay it all out and tell it how it is. I sighed again. "You know I hate this stuff…but give it here." I took Mike's phone, looked at the video, and pressed play. For the next ten minutes I watched one of the goriest things I'd ever seen, grimacing and closing my eyes at certain parts. When it was over, I sat staring at the phone, trying to collect my thoughts on it.

"From the look on your face I'd say you didn't like it." Mike peeled his phone from my hands.

I looked at him, the grimace still in place. "And *you do*? That's one of your classmates I just watched being murdered. How can you even *think* of liking that?"

The huge grin on his face slid away as he realised what I'd said. "Yeah, dude." His tone was sombre. "Yeah, I do get that it's one of our classmates…but dude…" The grin was back. "The video is *awesome*."

*****

We were in last period when we saw a group of police escort someone through the school and out to the waiting squad car. We all eagerly clamoured at the window and watched Steve Biselle, with a panicked expression, being herded out and forced into the car.

"Steve Biselle," I murmured, puzzled as to why he was the one they picked.

"Yeah, dude," Mike replied. "He was dating Maybelle. It's only been going a couple of weeks, but word is," he flashed a cheeky grin, "he does it cause she gives out and gives him…you-know-whats."

I watched the car drive away with a frown. "What are, you-know-whats?"

"Dude." He punched my right arm, making me look at his serious face. "*You-know-whats*". He wiggled his brows for effect.

I shook my head. "Nope, don't know what you-know-whats means."

"Oh, for God's sake." Janelle rolled her eyes beside us. "You may be educated in the ways of the world, Jordan, but definitely *not* in sex ed. He's talking about oral sex. Blow jobs, head jobs,

whatever you want to call it. 'You-know-whats'."
She made quotation marks with her fingers.

"And *that* is probably why Maybelle had the
word 'whore' written on her chest," Mike added as
we all went back to our seats. "She gives out to the
head jock and the killer thinks she's a whore for it.
The pictures are all over the internet, and you can
clearly see the killer writing it on her chest in her
own blood."

"Can you?" I hadn't really noticed much in the
video and was trying to forget what I had seen.

Mike shook his head. "Dude, you *really* need to
be more aware of what's going on online. Open
your eyes a little more."

"Not if online looks like that I don't."

The bell sounded, and after being told we'd be
back to normal tomorrow, we all filed out of class
and to the bus stop.

"Wonder what will happen to him." Janelle
stood beside us. "If he'll be charged I mean."

"Unless they have evidence to back their charges,
he won't be," I replied.

*****

Two days later, Steve was back at school and
surprisingly different. The once brash, loud, and
arrogant twelfth grader had been reduced to a quiet,
shy, stick-to-himself kinda guy.

Mike and I stood watching him in the hallway.
"Dude, he's changed." Mike shook his head. "Just

last week I heard him bragging to his mates how he'd scored with Maybelle, how he *rode her*, and now…he's just…a shell of his former self."

I closed my locker door and glanced at Mike. "I guess being accused of murder and questioned about the death of your girlfriend can change a man."

"Or." Mike whipped his phone out of his jean pocket. "It's because he's had his name added to the badluck-youredead death list." He brought up the website and clicked the menu. "Here, look. He's top of that list."

I reluctantly looked at the page and saw the name, Steve Biselle, front and centre. Next to it was a note that read, *'for the rape and murder of Maybelle Ryder'*. "Whoa," I murmured. "He hasn't even been charged with anything and someone's calling for his death because of a murder he didn't commit?"

Mike looked at me curiously. "How do *you* know he didn't commit it?"

I became a little smug. "Because if he was charged with murder he wouldn't be here at school." Sometimes it was so easy being a know-it-all when you knew it all.

"Mmm, well…hey, Janelle's moving in on him."

We watched Janelle sidle up to Steve and start talking to him; a sympathetic hand on his arm, a casual hair flick behind the ear, a shy smile on her face. He responded with a shy smile of his own and a small nod, then they walked together up the hall.

"What's she up to?" we murmured at the same time.

"Whoa, dude." Mike's eyes widened. "She couldn't wait to get on *that* bandwagon. Hitting on him already when he was only questioned two days ago."

"Clearly she didn't think that much of Maybelle," I added as we walked toward class. "If she's hitting on the boyfriend already then maybe…" I stopped. "Maybe she got rid of Maybelle so Steve was free for her." I nodded in excitement. "Janelle wanted Steve all along, so got rid of her competition."

Mike joined in the excitement. "And she always complained that Maybelle was beating her at choir. Always getting leads, and being front and centre and everything."

"Well." I started walking again. "Looks like there's a *second* suspect in the case."

CHAPTER THREE

The next morning we didn't see Janelle or Steve until lunchtime.

"I *cannot* believe I was hauled into the cop station this morning for questioning." Janelle slumped down in a chair at our table and covered her face with her hands. "Now they think *I* did it," she wailed, drawing surprised looks from the students around us.

"Keep acting like that and we'll all think you're guilty." I took a bite of apple.

She glared at me. "How *dare you*, Jordan Belmont. Me? *Me?* Guilty of murdering a classmate?" She flung her arms wide to emphasise her words. "It could have been *any* of us." That surprised and angered those sitting around us. "Oh, don't look so surprised," she told them. "*None* of you liked Maybelle; it could have been *any* of you." She turned and pointed at me. "Even *you*, Jordan Belmont. *You* could have done it. *Any of us* could have done it. Or *none* of us could have done it!"

"Grandstanding and blaming others only makes you look guiltier," I replied, watching her squirm at my words.

She calmed down and leaned on the table. "Do *you guys* think it was me? *Seriously,* do you think *I* did it?" She looked from me to Mike and back again.

"Well…" Mike and I answered at the same time.

"You did hate her for being better than you at choir," Mike finished.

"You hit on Steve two days after she was found dead," I added. *"Her boyfriend!"*

Janelle glared daggers at me. "Is *that* what this is about?" she hissed. "I offer my condolences to a boy who just lost his girlfriend who I was in choir with and *I'm* suddenly the wicked witch hitting on grieving ex-boyfriends?"

I shrugged. "When you put it like that then…yes."

Janelle slammed her chair back as she stood up. "Well, if *that's* the way you plan on thinking Jordan Belmont, *we* are no longer friends." She stormed off.

"We were friends?" I called after her, puzzled by her comment.

"Well, *I* definitely don't see us as friends," Mike said. "We're just classmates." He pulled his phone out and checked badluck-youredead. "Whoa. Janelle's name has gone from one hundred to number two on the death list. And there's a note…*for killing Maybelle Ryder so she can have Steve Biselle all to herself*. Whoa."

I shook my head. "One hundred? How many are on that list?"

Mike scrolled down. "Looks like just about everyone

from this school." He laughed loudly. "Even *you* made the list. You're 4071, and the reason is for being a nerd and a goody two shoes. Looks like someone wants *you* dead, Jordan."

*****

Tuesday morning we were at assembly again, and Principal Schaeffer called for silence before making his announcement. "I regret to inform you that, uh…" He cleared his throat. "Steve Biselle has been found dead in the woods at the back of his home, late yesterday afternoon." He wiped his mouth. "This, ah, means that the police want to talk to you again to find out who saw him last."

"Did someone kill him or did he kill himself because of Maybelle?" a voice called from the crowd.

The Principal raised his hand. "We will not be discussing such things until the police have informed us about what's going on."

"No," whispered a voice beside us. We turned to see Janelle, rocking back and forth, her head moving side to side. "No," she whispered again. "No, no, no, no, no." The pitch of her voice escalated as she ran across the gym and out the door. Teachers and police followed her.

I frowned. "I wonder if she'll still be a suspect?"

"Why would she be?" Mike pulled out his phone. "Her potential love interest just died, she ends up with nothing. If he was still alive she'd have him, but dead…she don't."

I noticed others were checking their phones and within a minute there were gasps around the gym. "What's going on?" I was the only one without a phone.

"Dude…it's online…"

I stared at Mike's white face. "What is?" Leaning over, I looked at the video on his phone. "Is that…?"

"Yep," breathed Mike. "Oh, my god, he hung himself."

We watched the body of Steve Biselle swing back and forth from a tree.

"Hanged. Mmm, so now we know it was suicide," I murmured.

Mike looked at me with a glazed over expression. "Dude…if he killed himself, then how did he write *'big cheat, small dick'* on his chest?"

We looked at the video closely and Mike pressed pause when Steve's naked body swung around. Those words were definitely on his chest.

I shrugged with disinterest. "Maybe he wrote it on before hanging himself?"

"Or, maybe someone killed him and made it look like suicide?" Mike said as the bell rang and we were herded back to class.

*****

At lunchtime everyone gathered around in small groups, phones in hands, watching the videos on badluck-youredead.com.

I really didn't understand the fascination with

watching videos of people dying. "*Why?*" I asked no one in particular as I glanced around the school. "*Why* are you all so involved and desperate to watch these videos? Watch your classmates drawing their last breath on earth?" I was an avid reader, and while I read about death and destruction, watching videos of people dying is where I draw the line. I gazed at the faces of my fellow classmates and those from other grades. Shock, disbelief, sadness, tears, crying.

I found Janelle surrounded by some of Steve's jock classmates, consoling her, a sympathetic hand on her arm, a casual hair flick, a shy smile on their faces. She responded with a shy smile of her own and a small nod then they all walked off together toward one of the school's sheds.

"And so it goes," I said. "The cycle continues."

"What you say…?" Mike threw a quick glance before looking at his phone again.

I shook my head. "*Why* are you watching that again? How many times is that now? Ten?" I tried to take the phone away, but Mike held on.

"More like fifty," he replied, finally getting some air. His eyes were wide and red tinged. "You see something different every time. Like one minute he has his shirt on then it's off. One minute he's alive and then he's hanging lifeless." He breathed in and out. "*Why* didn't he fight? He's the jock of the school and football captain. He had muscles, was over six foot tall. *Why* didn't he fight?" Mike frowned. "*None* of this makes sense if it's suicide."

"How can it be when the camera caught him swaying?" I wondered if these videos were like crack cocaine for Mike, considering the way he looked. "If he set up the camera you would have seen him hang himself. You don't. So he clearly didn't hang himself."

"So you agree with me then? He didn't kill himself. It wasn't suicide."

"Not from seeing that video fifty times. No, it wasn't suicide." I watched Janelle and the group of jocks emerge from behind the shed. The bell rang and she quickly wiped her mouth and pulled down her uniform while two jocks zipped up their pants.

"And so it goes," I said. "The cycle continues."

CHAPTER FOUR

Thursday morning we noticed Janelle and those same jocks weren't at school, and while we heard the whisperings of other students, we also knew it more than likely wasn't them who killed Maybelle or Steve. Not to discount the jocks for being jealous because Steve was top jock, or Janelle for being jealous of Maybelle for being better at choir. It just seemed highly unlikely that it was them. We checked the badluck-youredead website at lunchtime and found Janelle was now number one on the death list.

"Well, why not?" I asked. "Steve's gone, so no need for him to be on that list anymore." I munched on my ham and tomato sandwich as Mike perused the site on his tablet.

"There are a lot of people on here…members I mean. I wonder if they're all from our school." Mike checked a few more pages. "Ah, it's divided up into schools, but somehow you can only view your own and no one else's. Wonder how they did that?"

"Have you signed up?"

He gave me a quick glance. "Um, yeah. I have."

"What details do they ask for?" I swallowed a mouthful of soda.

"Um…username, password, state, school, postcode…"

"There you go then." I got up and dumped my rubbish in the bin before grabbing my bag. "You put in what school you go to so there's probably some algorithm or code that prevents you from looking at other schools."

Mike looked up in surprise. "How do *you* know that?"

I rolled my eyes. "We study computer science, Mike, not hard to figure out when you know what goes into making a website."

He nodded. "Yeah, that's it. Guess I was asleep when we learned that stuff, but then you always ace that class anyway."

I smiled smugly. "I ace *everything*, Mike. *Every* class."

He started saying something then grabbed my arm. "Look, it's Janelle."

I turned and watched her walk from the car park, across the quad, and into the office with her mother. Neither looked happy.

"Mmm, wonder what that's about?" Mike quickly looked at the website again before putting his tablet away. "Having a chat with the Principal are we?"

"Clearly it's long overdue," I replied.

*****

Janelle didn't make it to class on Friday either, neither did the jocks, the *supposed* best friends of Steve Biselle. Rumours flew thick and fast about all of them. Why had Janelle come in with her mother? What was it about? Why wasn't she there? Why weren't the jocks there? Had any been arrested and charged, or were they just taking a few days off school to get away from the prying eyes and questions of their fellow students?

Of course, they weren't the only rumours flying around as there had been a change on the badluck-youredead website. Janelle was still number one on the death list, but the note beside her name had changed. It now read, *'underage whore who gives head to dead men who murder their girlfriends'*. And the jocks' names had all moved up to numbers 2 through 6 with some notes of, *'likes little girls who give head, never mind the fact they're underage and it's illegal'*.

We mused over the changes.

"It's *got* to be someone at this school." Mike scrolled through the rest of the list. "They *clearly* know details."

"Didn't you say you can add the names yourself?" I scrounged in my bag for my chemistry book. "So whoever put their names on it must've changed the notes?" I found it and flicked through to the page we needed for that afternoon's test.

"Yeah…I guess. If we can upload and add stuff, and add people to the list as well as go into the forums and chat, then yeah, all the comments are by us." He looked at me. "Well, by *us*, not *you*, *you're* not on social media. Have you even checked out this site?"

"Still not interested." I turned over the page. "Are you going to study for the exam today, or live on that website?"

"Is there any point in me studying when you always ace the test and are top of the class anyway?" His fingers flew over the screen.

I smiled and glanced at him. "If you studied you would have the ability to beat me…*potentially.*"

"Dude." Mike looked up from his tablet. "*No one* can beat you at chemistry. Or computer science, or health, or anything else we do. *You're* Mr Know-it-all."

"Not quite." I think my attempt at being humble failed.

"Dude, *quite.*" Mike shook his head. "You're like a brainiac computer that remembers everything it sees, hears and reads."

"Not quite," I mumbled, thinking about everything I still needed to learn. "Not quite."

*****

Our class found out on Monday morning that Janelle would not be coming back for the rest of the term. Her parents thought it would be best to stay away and regroup. Rumours had her in some sort of mental facility. I knew for a fact that she was home because she lives a few streets away from us.

And Mike had rung her to see if she needed help with any work she'd been given to do.

The jocks were back at school. Andy Siddell, Bo Drew, Joe Best, Peter Jones, and Will Holden all looked like hell frozen over. Pale complexions, sunken eyes, quiet, and desperately needing to hide from prying eyes. Eyes that stared and glared and accused and abused. The boys kept to themselves as much as possible, preferring to stay in the library at lunchtime so they wouldn't be harassed.

"Do we know if anyone's been charged with Maybelle's murder and Steve's…whatever it was?" I asked Mike during our free class. We were sitting in the library trying to get some work done. Well, I was. Mike was scrolling through social media looking for pics of our dead classmates.

"Whoa." He stopped at one site. "There's a whole bunch of comments about the jocks and they ain't good. Listen to this. *'#murderer Andy Siddell likes little girls sucking his cock', '#murderer Bo Drew is a muff muncher', '#murderer Joe Best actually prefers little boys'.*" He looked up in the disbelief which had been going around a lot for the last week or so. "This stuff's nasty. Narst-ay!"

"One *could* question whether it's deserved or not." I flipped through some papers. "If you're going to partake not only in illegal underage activity, but social media as well, then you better be prepared for what happens if your privates get out across the internet." I stood so I could lean across the big table to spread my papers out and order them properly. "You do stupid things you're gonna get caught. And there is *always* a backlash that goes with it. Psychology 101."

"What? Are you studying psychology in your spare time?" Mike joked. "'Cause we don't have that here. But…" he paused. "You might be right about keeping your privates private. *Why* do people put so much stuff over the internet?"

"Why do *you* look at so much stuff like that?" I sat back down. "*You* tell *me*. You're all over it. I'm not."

CHAPTER FIVE

Tuesday morning we found out that *none* of them would be coming back to school. For the third week running, we all crowded into the gym and sat down to listen to Principal Schaeffer tell us that another of our classmates was dead. And not just one. Janelle and her five jocks were all found in densely forested parklands in the early hours of the morning and the police were out in force. A very *big* force. I counted one hundred of them lined around the wall of the gym. Watching us, waiting for us, any of us, to slip up and make a move.

Wait…I've been watching way too many TV crime dramas.

"Whoa, dude," Mike breathed. "This is *so not good.*"

A policeman with multiple stripes on his sleeve walked to the front of the room. "I am Superintendent Davis. We will be thoroughly speaking to each and every one of you to find out what you know. When you last saw them. When you last spoke to them. We are treating this series of deaths as murders, which means we have a serial killer on the loose and he's targeting schoolkids. We also want to stress that you *do not* go out after dark, you *do not* go anywhere alone, and you let *someone* know where you'll be every second of the day if you want to stay alive," he boomed and motioned to the officers. "Now, each officer will take a class and personally interview each of you. I suggest you tell the truth and be as honest as possible. Lying and deceiving us will not get you anywhere, and it certainly won't catch the killer." He stood back as the Principal took to the mic.

"Everyone, please, follow your teacher back to your room and an officer will be around shortly."

We filed out of the gym and Mike quickly pulled out his phone. Scrolling through badluck-youredead he found a video for the murders. "Whoa…"

"Now what?" I craned my neck to see what he was watching and then noticed others had done the same.

"Oh, my God, that's disgusting."

"Ew, gross. What a whore."

"Oh, dude, he's getting some pussy."

I grabbed Mike's phone and hit replay. We stopped to watch the video and I wasn't sure what I was seeing. Janelle and the jocks sat around a campfire. It looked like they were drinking, kissing, touching, then Janelle pulled her dress off and lay down. One by one, in between drinking and what looked like smoking, each jock lay on top of Janelle and they screwed while another seemed to sit on her face. But he obscured the view.

"Dude, they all had sex with her and is she blowing them off at the same time?" Mike was peering over my shoulder.

"Boys, come along," Mrs Mendoza called. We quickly caught up, ran into our classroom, and sat down. Looking at the video, we saw they were now lying around, not moving, slumped over logs, or Janelle.

The scene changed, and they were all naked and lying in a semi-circle around Janelle, who still had a jock on top of her. The camera moved toward the campfire and we saw them perfectly still and naked.

There was one word written on four jock's chests. *Dead. Men. Tell. No...* and on the back of the fifth, who was lying on Janelle, was the word, *Tales*.

The screen went black.

With hearts racing we looked at each other. "Whoa…"

"That's enough," snapped Mrs Mendoza and we jumped. "Turn that damned thing off and give it to me." She walked over to us with her hand out. "You'll get it back at home time."

With a bright red shamed face, Mike reluctantly handed it over. Every other kid with a phone had to do the same. Mrs Mendoza put them in her desk drawer as the officer called the first victim…uh, student.

We spent the next few hours quietly chatting or reading, as there was no point doing any work as it would always be interrupted.

At lunchtime, Mike grabbed his tablet from his bag and went to badluck-youredead while we conferred on what we were asked.

"Sounds like we were asked the same thing." I unwrapped my sandwich. "Last to see them, talk to them, how well did we know them? Did you tell the cop you called Janelle?"

"Did *you* tell them you saw her the other day?" Mike played the video. "You live closer to her. You saw her from the window didn't you? Did you tell them?"

"Yep." I swallowed. "I told them what I know and saw."

Mike did a hashtag search through social media. "Oh, my God. I wonder if the cops know about *this*?" He held the tablet in front of my face as I took another bite of chicken and tomato. "'*Whores tell all*'," I read aloud. The words were written on Janelle's naked torso, presumably in blood since that seemed to be what the killer did. Something stirred and tingled in my privates at the sight of Janelle's bare breasts. I swallowed. "Get that out of my face, I'm eating." I pushed it aside and grabbed my soda. Sculling back half, I felt the private stirrings subside.

"Wait." The puzzlement in Mike's voice made me look at him. He flicked through a few websites and back and forth between pages. "How was that photo taken if Andy was lying on top of her in the video?"

I shrugged. "He wrote it on her chest before

putting Andy on top of her?"

"But in this video it looks like he's still…you know…"

I raised a brow waiting to see how he'd finish that sentence.

He made obscene hand gestures. "*You* know… inside of her. So how'd he write on their bodies if Andy was still on top?"

I thought about it. "He could have written on Andy's back and then partly rolled him off, or moved him to write on her chest—"

"Dude must be strong then."

"Must be…"

The photos soon caught everyone's attention, and once again rumours and gossip spread like wildfire. You couldn't say it wasn't going to, of course it was. Five naked jocks screwing an underage naked fifteen year old schoolmate in what we now found out was a drug and alcohol-fuelled party.

The news websites had every detail they could get out about it, and even told torrid stories dragging Maybelle and Steve back into it. Underage kids, sex, drugs, rock 'n roll, even going as far as to claim they were forcing girls against their will. Not that Janelle looked like she was being forced. Little did they know why it was really happening.

The rest of the week was sombre and morose. A lot of kids stayed home, but I got on with it. It's not that I wasn't emotional. I just didn't have time for bad people who did bad things.

CHAPTER SIX

"And so we lay Maybelle Jane Ryder, and Steve Marcus Biselle, to rest. May God take care of them and their souls."

Organ music swelled among the rooftops as we all stood to bid goodbye to the bodies of our classmates. Gazing around the church, I saw year ten, eleven, and twelve classmates crying or trying to hold it together.

Dressed in our black suits, Mike and I slowly wandered up the middle aisle, past the coffins of a blue suited Steve, and a pink dressed Maybelle, and down the side aisle to the front door. I quickly stepped outside and took a huge gulp of fresh air. "God I can't breathe."

"No need to get melodramatic." Mike stood beside me, hands in pockets, a sombre expression on his fifteen-year-old face.

I shrugged nonchalantly. "I hate churches. I think they're stuffy." I loosened my tie. "And I can't breathe with this thing on."

We stood silently and watched our peers file out

and then hover nearby, waiting for the families to emerge. They had decided to share the funeral service so their children could be on display for all of their classmates to attend. The police had kept the bodies until two days ago when the Ryders and Biselles claimed them.

"Nice of them to have it on a Saturday so we could come." Mike's voice was soft as he moved nervously in place. "But I'm not sure I want to be here anymore."

I agreed with Mike. "We can go now, we don't need to stay." Besides, no doubt we'd be attending another service in the coming weeks.

Mike's parents had driven us and now picked us up and drove us home. We went up to his room and he turned on the PC, logging into badluck-youredead.com.

I groaned. "Haven't you had enough of that? When are you going to *stop obsessing* with it?" I threw myself on his bed and ripped off my tie.

"I can't." He clicked the mouse. "Something's not right and I need to figure it out."

"Figure *what* out?" I stared at the glow-in-the-dark stars on the ceiling.

"*Who's* doing this? *Why* they're doing it. *Why them*?" A few more clicks and he was watching the Janelle and jocks video again.

I sighed. "If you're going to be this boring I may as well go." I sat up only to be ignored by my best friend. Adding another sigh I walked out the door.

Monday morning the newspapers had it all. The

forensic testing was done and the results were in. Janelle and the jocks had been drugged, or were doing drugs, and didn't know what harm they could, *or would,* do. It was some sort of drug used to knock people out, basically making them unable to move, and some other drug that was lethal in large doses. And large doses they were.

The reports also claimed that Janelle had sex with all five boys and had died during the deed with Andy. The words were written in their own blood, or should I say, own flesh, as they were carved into their skin post mortem. That means after death.

I stopped by the newsagent after school and bought as many papers as I could. This was getting interesting.

And fortunately Tuesday morning came and went with no announcement. No murder. No death, no more classmates killed, no more police at our door.

Mike and I talked over lunch. "I can't believe we haven't had a death yet." He scrolled through social media.

"How come you don't have lunch anymore? I don't think I've seen you eat in three weeks, since we heard about Maybelle." I munched down on a beef and cheese sandwich. I know, I was rather plain and boring in my food choices. I got no answer so I gave him a nudge.

"Huh?" He looked up in surprise.

"How come you don't eat lunch anymore?" I repeated.

He shrugged. "Not interested in food when this stuff is happening. Here, look." He moved his tablet. "Their names have disappeared."

"They *are* dead. No need to keep their names up when the deed is done."

He gave me a strange look. "But look *here*." He pointed to the comment attached to the video of Janelle. "The message has changed."

"'*Dead boys tell no tales, dead whores tell it all, dead boys aren't yet males, dead whores know the score. You play with fire you're gonna burn to the core*'." I pulled a face. "Ugh, whatever. It doesn't even make sense."

Mike agreed. "Yeah, I know, but clearly the person changing all the messages is trying to leave some clue as to why they're doing this."

I cocked an eyebrow. "Really? *That's* what you think?"

His head bounced up and down eagerly. "Maybelle was giving Steve perks and twerks, Steve blabbed all about it. With Maybelle dead, her biggest rival, Janelle, had a free pass to Steve. But with Steve dead, that gave his jealous jock mates a free pass to Janelle. And judging from this video…" He replayed it. "…they passed it hard and fast and she clearly didn't refuse."

"No, she didn't," I muttered, finishing off my lunch. "So, what next, Sherlock? Have you deduced who's doing it and why?"

Mike stared at the screen. "I don't know who," he said slowly. "But maybe the why has something to do with underage sex, or bad morals, or something."

That piqued my interest. "You mean someone's killing kids because they have no morals, and the person doing it wants to teach them a lesson?"

He shrugged. "I don't know. Just thinking out loud."

The bell rang loud and long.

"You'll have to think out loud later 'cause right now we've got class."

*****

Thursday morning during recess, Mike had that damned tablet back in his hand.

"Haven't you had enough yet?" I watched one of our teachers stroll up to a group of girls sitting on the grass. He crouched down, close to one of the oldest, and spoke to them. I'm not a lip reader, so I have no idea what he was saying, but a few moments later they laughed. Wow. My brow furrowed. He made them laugh. He gently touched the oldest girl on the shoulder and got to his feet. She blushed, and he did a little finger wave before walking away.

"What's *her* name," I asked Mike. "Do you know who those girls are?" I pointed in their direction.

After having a good look he told me. "Kristen Thomas is the oldest, she's year eleven. Then there's Sally Meters on her right and Michelle Myers on *her* right. They're year elevens too. I think there's two year tens and a year nine. Don't know their names." He went back to his tablet.

*****

At lunch, he shoved it in my face again. "Look at all the posts on the forums. People are really letting rip on our classmates and saying all sorts of things."

I studied my biology book, my sandwich in mid-air. "I guess it *would* be pretty bad. I don't think any of them were too well liked."

"Not according to these comments. Geez, I wonder if it's kids we know posting this stuff?" We both looked up and around. The ones we could see had phones or tablets up and working. I spied the group of girls from earlier looking in the direction of the teacher. Biology teacher, that's it. Mr... Smooth. No, that can't be it. Mr... I frowned when he smiled and gave a little finger wave at Kristen. She gave one back with a little giggle and her face went red when the others teased her.

He headed in their direction, hands clasped behind his back, chatting with other kids until he reached them. The other girls left, leaving Kristen alone with him. There was a sympathetic hand on her arm, a casual hair flick, a shy smile on his face. She imitated his actions as he did them. A light touch on his arm, a flick of the hair behind her ear, a shy smile on *her* face.

"And so it goes," I muttered in irritation. "The cycle continues."

"What's that?"

"Mmm?"

"You say something?"

"No."

"I've checked a lot of usernames and can't see any that might be other kids here. We probably all used a name we couldn't be identified by."

"Did you?" I finished off my sandwich and reached for an orange.

"Of course. I'm not stupid." His pride sounded injured.

"Then the other kids clearly aren't either."

He pulled a face while he thought. "True. I wonder who the person uploading all the videos is."

"Is there a name?"

"It just says admin, so I guess whoever owns or runs the site is doing it."

"Well, that's a mystery then." The bell rang. "Let's go to biology."

I watched Mr Smooth pace back and forth across the room as he told us about the birds and the bees. For a man of thirty-two, it couldn't have been easy talking to fifteen year olds about sex. No wonder he was pacing. He couldn't look any of us in the eye.

"So." He stopped. "Do you need to see the video?"

No one answered, except me.

"I'd say we've seen Janelle and the jocks campfire video enough to know what sex is, Mr Smooth. Maybe you should tell us how it's illegal to have underage sex as any male over eighteen can be charged with statutory rape if arrested." I watched him squirm as some of the kids tittered in the background. "You know the laws about underage sex don't you, Mr Smooth? If you don't, I could tell everyone. I'm well informed, considering so much of it seems to be going on amongst the kids here at school." I was deadly serious and could see my biology teacher had absolutely nothing to say from embarrassment.

Mike nudged me under our table, but the bell rang before anyone moved.

Our teacher got a hold of himself. "Please read your biology books for your next class on Tuesday." He gave me a queer look. "I'll see you next week."

I followed Mike and the others out of the room.

"Dude…whoa…what *was* that…?" Mike crowed. "You *really* stuck it to him. I'd be surprised if you don't get into trouble." We reached our lockers and grabbed books for the next class.

"Get into trouble for what?" I replaced my biology book with my chemistry. "For wanting to state the law about underage sex? That's what the class is about. Sex and biology. May as well address the laws about it at the same time." I shut my locker and we walked off. "Besides, that's what was going on between Maybelle and Steve and Janelle and the jocks. Underage sex. We need to talk about the laws that go with it."

CHAPTER SEVEN

On Friday I kept an eye on Mr Smooth, watching him at recess and lunch. He came close to making a move on, Kristen but always noticed me watching. So did Kristen, who got irritated every time the teacher saw her, then saw me, and quickly turned away.

She came storming toward us before lunch was over. "Who the hell do you think you are spying on me? Spying on Mr Smooth? Are you jealous or something? Want a piece of this arse for yourself do you?" She bent over and flipped her dress uniform up past her backside which she wiggled. "Well, you ain't getting a piece of *this* arse. Oh, wait." She straightened and touched her forefinger to her chin in thought. "Maybe you want a piece of *Mr Smooth's* arse instead? Is that what it is, gay boy? You want *his arse* instead?" Her followers had gathered nearby and now giggled. So did everyone else that was sitting in earshot.

I went beet red. I know I did, so I needed a snappy reply. "Unless you want to end up like

Maybelle and Janelle I suggest you keep your dress down, your knickers up, your mouth shut, and your eyes off an adult male who's not only too old for you, which would make it rape, but who seems to forget it's highly illegal for a teacher to have sex with a student."

Her jaw dropped, and like everyone else, she just stared at me.

I stood proudly; basking in my triumphant state then added this low blow. "Nice blue floral undies by the way." I walked away to shrieks of laughter.

*****

On Monday, I kept an eye on Kristen and Mr Smooth. Mike didn't share my worries; he was more interested in tracking down the owner of badluck-youredead.com, and maybe in the process, finding the killer.

I knew something was up, and didn't want any more classmates to end up dead. It was, and is, bad enough to deal with one or two, but *eight,* in *three weeks.* That was just horrific.

I watched the furtive glances between Kristen and our biology teacher at recess. They steered clear of each other, but that changed at lunchtime. With even more furtive glances, I saw Mr Smooth make a small head movement at Kristen. He then walked off and a few seconds later she followed. A few seconds later *I* followed, leaving my lunch, and Mike, with his head stuck in his tablet.

I trailed after her and saw Smooth go into the tech building. A few seconds later Kristen followed. A few seconds later *I* followed, but neither was to be seen. I looked around and quietly moved into the room.

I heard a sound come from somewhere to my left and headed for the doorway. There were three doors branching off, one on my left, one on my right, and the one in front of me that was partly open.

Another noise…

Muffled voices came from the behind the door in front of me and I stepped closer, putting my ear to the one inch gap to hear what was happening.

"Mmm, mmm, oh, Kristen. I want you so much, mmm…"

My brows flew up in disbelief even though I had suspected it. *Seriously? Right here in the school? Yuck!*

"Oh, Dick, I want you too…mmm…"

Dick? Oh, God please tell me his name's *not* Dick Smooth. I heard the rustling of clothing and moved to peek inside and saw them leaning against a bench.

Kristen's uniform was pushed up to her waist, her knickers down around one ankle, her legs locked around a half-naked Dick Smooth whose pants and jocks were around his ankles.

"Uh, oh, uh, mmm…" They groaned and grunted in unison as Dick thrust back and forth into Kristen.

Bannngggg. A door slammed somewhere in the building.

I jumped back in fright, scared that I'd been seen.

"Quick, hurry, get dressed," Dick said. "I'll see you tonight."

With the rustling of more clothes, I silently got the hell out of there.

*****

It was Tuesday once again and, after having a reprieve for two weeks, we were back to where we started five weeks ago. Back to sitting in the gym listening to the Principal and Superintendent of Police tell us about another death. Another *student* death. But this was different. There was also a man dead. That man was our biology teacher. Dick Smooth was dead. I guess Dick wasn't so smooth after all. Kristen Thomas was dead. They were dead, together, bound forever by an arrow through their chests.

I glanced down at Mike's phone and watched the video again. Kristen and Dick having sex against a tree in one of the parks. An arrow shot out of the darkness, slicing and dicing its way through Dick's back and Kristen's front, pinning them to the tree forever. For all eternity. Or until they stopped shuddering. The camera moved closer, capturing their stunned expressions, making sure to zoom in on their entwined sexual organs, showing a grown adult male having sex with an underage child. Showing a teacher having sex with his student. The scene stopped and changed. Now they were naked, and in what I assumed was blood, were the words, *'I like little girls'*, on Dick's back.

"Whoa," Mike said. "Look at the comments, and look." He scrolled to the death list. "They weren't even on the list."

"Maybe they were a last minute thing," I suggested as we shuffled out the door. "Maybe no one thought that would happen, so there was no need to put their names on it." We reached our class. "Besides, who would have known about Mr Smooth…?"

*****

Friday afternoon we were in the library for a double period and Mike had papers all over the table. "We've got to be able to figure it out." He excitedly shuffled and moved papers around. "Here..." He pointed to the top left one. "This is the date the website started, those are the lists of schools that are supposedly on the site, here's a list of what info you need to become a user." He pointed to another. "Here's a printout of all the victims' names being on the death list except for Kristen and Mr Smooth, and here's a timeline of when the murders were committed. But get this." He sat down when he saw the librarian's evil eye pointed at him. "They were all murdered on a Monday night and found sometime during Tuesday." He grabbed my arm. "So the killer has a thing for Mondays. I wonder what that is." He shoved his head back in his paperwork.

I left him to his wonderings and moved to another table.

CHAPTER EIGHT

I was in my basement on Monday afternoon when Mike galloped down the stairs. For a few seconds I freaked out because no one knew about the basement except my family, and I had certainly never told anyone that my office was down there, and I had certainly never invited anyone over, especially Mike, in the entire time I'd known him. I quickly recovered when he stopped dead in the middle of the room with his jaw hanging open.

I stopped as well and watched his facial expressions. His eyes scoured every inch of the four walls in my basement. They were covered in maps, newspaper articles, printouts of articles, photos, personal details, anything and everything about the murders, our classmates and who potential killers were. Oh, and coloured string to join all the dots.

"Whoa…dude…" he managed. "This is more than I printed out and put together." His eyes scanned back and forth, his head moving in unison.

I waited, nervous, palms sweating, tongue drying out.

He stepped closer, reading everything I had on the walls. *"How did you get all this stuff? Why* do you have all this stuff?" He finally turned to look at me, disbelief and shock all over his face.

I shrugged. "Well," I replied, calm now. "When you mentioned doing it for an assignment, I thought, why not. Besides, with a lawyer for a mother, and a forensic scientist for a father, it seemed only natural to try and figure it out and use it for my end of year assignment." The lie flowed smoothly from my tongue, but then again, maybe I *would* use it for my end of year assignment.

Mike nodded. "Yeah, I get that. I forgot about your parents. Yeah, bet they had somethin' to say about all this stuff being in the news and all."

"Yes. We've had a lot of discussions about it. In fact, they wholeheartedly agreed about the assignment." My eyes followed Mike as he moved along the wall. "And they offer great advice when needed."

"Yeah…I bet they do." He nodded in agreement and stopped. "Hey, where'd you get this information from?" He pointed to a paper on the wall outlining the details of Dick and Kristen's death. "I didn't read any of that in the paper or online."

"Well…as I said, my mother's a lawyer…" I let the sentence trail off hoping he would pick it up.

His eyes widened. "She's been getting stuff for you?" I smiled. "That is so cool." He kept moving around the room and I stood wondering how the hell my mother could let him in, or tell him I was in the basement. She knew that was my sanctuary, my office, my free space to express myself as I saw fit. And now, I had to worry about blabbermouth Mike and him not keeping quiet.

"Hey, is that a list of the chemicals found in the alcohol Janelle and the jocks drank? How do you have that? Oh wait." He pointed at me and smiled. "Forensic scientist for a dad, and you're the ace chem dude, top of our class, always getting As." Another pause, but this time with a jealous look. "Teacher's pet." He turned back to the wall and I slowly walked up behind him.

"Yes, well, with a forensic scientist for a father it was a safe bet I'd be good at chemistry, amongst other things."

His head moved up and down. "Yeah, they must make you excel at everything?"

I tilted my head and thought about it. "Yes… everything. The family that plays together stays together." I silently covered my video camera and switched off my PC.

"You even printed out all of the social media stuff. I thought you weren't online?"

"I'm not. But just because I'm not on it, doesn't mean I can't track it down and see it…or print it out for an assignment." I sneaked up behind him. "Boo," I yelled, making him jump ten feet in the air.

"Ah, gah, you scared me." He grabbed his heaving chest.

I laughed. "You sissy. You are *way* too involved in this. You need to get a life."

He looked around as his breathing returned to

normal. "What, like *you*?"

I shrugged again. "This *is* my life."

His faced showed several expressions at once, but I couldn't grab onto what they were and I doubt he could figure out what he was feeling either. Finally, he spoke. "Have you checked the net today?" He pulled his phone out. "There's nothing new on badluck-youredead, but the comments are still coming thick and fast."

"I printed some earlier. I'll do some more later." I gazed at my walls. "Gotta keep adding to it." I slyly glanced at him. "It all goes into making a *great* assignment."

Mike rolled his eyes. "Is work all you ever think about?"

I smiled. "Not all."

"Yeah, well, can I get some pics or photocopies or something so I can work on it at home?" He managed to get a few quick snaps before I pushed his hand down.

"Do your own dirty work," I joked. "This took me weeks. Besides, *I* want all the credit." I started shoving him towards the stairs. "Time to go. I've got work to do."

"Yeah, yeah," he mumbled, making his way up the stairs. "See you tomorrow."

"Yeah." I heard the front door slam. "I'll definitely be seeing *you* tomorrow."

*****

Strangely, Mike seemed determined to avoid me at school. He ignored me on the bus when I said hello, and sat as far away from me during class as he could. I didn't even see him during recess or lunch, and he teamed up with another kid for sport.

I finally cornered him on the bus home. "For Pete's sake, why have you avoided me all day? Have I got the plague or something? Do I have b.o.?" I sniffed myself then looked at his face, hoping the lame joke would make him crack a smile. It didn't.

His eyes searched my face as if trying to find the answers to questions he didn't want to ask, and didn't want to know either.

I frowned. "Don't tell me you're jealous that I have inside info on the school murders and you don't?" I slumped back in my seat as we pulled up at our bus stop. "I can't help it if I have parents on the inside."

We got off and headed down our street. We lived on the same street, which was several kilometres long and had a strip of heavy dense scrub and forest running along behind the houses.

I looked at the trees towering over the rooftops. It was a nice view on a hot summer night, and could hide lots of things…like dead bodies.

I noticed Mike had barged ahead, head down, not looking back. I ran after him and grabbed his arm, spinning him around to face me.

"Spit it out, coward. Whatever you have to say have the decency to say it to my face. Why did you ignore me today?" I waited. I wanted to hear the answer I needed.

He gave me that funny searching look again. "You…*know* stuff…stuff *no one* else does…you have info *no one else* does…and details and parents, and know about chemistry and biology…" He shook his head. "Forget about it." He stalked off down the street.

I watched after him. Yes, I knew what needed to be done.

*****

I made my plan and waited until dark to execute it. Dressed completely in black, I walked stealthily through the bushland at the back of my house until I got to Mike's. His room was at the back and his light was on. I climbed up the tree beside the house and made my way over to his second floor window.

"Hey." I stuck my head through and saw him jump. I laughed and climbed on in. "Scared you." I took in all the paper on the wall. "Looks like you've done a lot of work yourself." I stepped closer to see what info he did have.

He backed up against a chest of drawers. "Yeah, well. I don't have experts for parents."

I glanced back at him. "You don't need experts for parents when there's so much available on Google." I moved toward him. "Being online can be so problematic. Don't you agree?"

He stayed silent, but sidled away. "What I said this afternoon, forget about it. It was just jealous ramblings as you said." He crossed his arms. "Look, my parents will be home soon, you'd better go. I've got lots of homework to do."

I wandered over to his baseball collection and casually picked up the bat. "The problem is, Mike..." I handled the smooth piece of wood in my hand as I turned around. "You know way too much."

CHAPTER NINE

Three hours later, I threw a bucket of water in Mike's face. He sputtered awake, flinging his head around and trying to open his eyes. "Welcome back." I stood in front of him. "Although, not for long."

He stared up at me. "What's happening? What's going on? Ugh." He shook his head. "What happened?"

"I hit you on the head with your bat," I replied simply.

He stared, dumbfounded. "Why? Why would you do that?"

I shrugged. "Because you know too much and had figured it out. Hadn't you?" I watched his expressions as I stepped aside. "You remember my parents, don't you?"

They were leaning against the desk and gave a little wave.

He shook his head again. "Um, hey, what's going on? Let me out of here. Help me. What's going on, Jordy?"

"It's Jordan," I spat. *"I always hated it when you*

called me that." I walked around him slowly. We had tied him to a chair which sat in the middle of the basement. The floor, walls and furniture now covered in plastic sheeting, and Mum, Dad and I were wearing those blue scientist onesie cover up suits you see them wear on CSI.

"Um, okay…sorry." He was clearly trying to sort everything out in his head.

"Come on, Mikey," I cajoled. "You already started getting it Sunday night didn't you? After being down here, which you never should have been, thanks Mum." I threw her a dirty look to which she shrugged her apology. "You started seeing things you hadn't seen before. All the info I had, the fact my parents know about crime, the fact that I excel at chem and biology amongst other things." I glanced at my parents. "It comes with the genes." I walked around again. "Come on, Mikey. Spit it out. You figured out that I had something to do with all of the murders, and that's why you avoided me like the plague." I waved a hand at Dad. "Not that we couldn't whip one up in our lab of course." He nodded in agreement. "You got it, Mikey." I stopped in front of him and leant down so we were face to face. "You got that it was me…"

He gulped and the expressions flew thick and fast over his face.

"It's true, Mikey."

His face crumpled. "It can't be," he sobbed. "It can't be."

"Why not? Why can't it be?"

"Because." Chokes racked his body.

"Because…" I encouraged.

His sobs became louder.

"Because?"

"Because you're my best friend."

The pain he must have been feeling hit me, because I was feeling it too. Mike had been my best friend since we were toddlers, but now, he had to go. For all our sakes. "I'm sorry, Mikey. I truly am." I moved away.

"What are you going to do with me?" he whimpered and frantically pulled at the rope around his hands, trying to free himself. Crying harder, he managed to wipe his face on his shoulder, and looking around, he didn't like what he saw. "What are you going to do?" His voice was now quiet and childish.

"We're going to kill you, Mikey." My answer was simple and to the point.

"Why?" So was his reply.

"Because you asked all the questions and figured out all the answers." I picked up my weapon of choice.

"No," he sobbed. "No I didn't. I didn't figure anything out, please, Jordy—"

I turned on him.

"Jordan," he corrected. "Please. I won't tell anyone, I promise. I won't. I don't know anything. I don't. I promise. I don't know anything…"

"Of course you do, Mikey. You saw everything on my walls." I picked up a pile of photos of a naked

Maybelle. "These photos that no one else could possibly have." I threw them into a bin. "Stupid me. I also gave you the idea about HTML and algorithms when it comes to setting up websites. Stupid me for being a computer whiz." I stared at the chemical compound print out. "You also know that I have private information about the drugs used to slow down and kill Janelle and the horny little jocks." I sneered at the thought of seeing them screw her while high as kites. "All thanks to Dad for that one." He gave a little wave.

I looked at Mike's confused expression. "Let me start from the beginning. You started getting too involved and asking questions you shouldn't have. Like why and who. You suggested it had something to do with underage sex and morals and bingo!" I clapped my hands in Mike's face. "You'd be right. They had no morals and I wanted to teach them a lesson. It all started with finding out about Maybelle. She was a horny little girl. Always dropping her undies for some boy, or dropping to her knees instead." I slowly walked around Mike. "So I decided to jump on the internet and post some stuff. That's how come I came up with www.badluck-youredead.com." I saw his surprised look. "Yes, Mike. That's me. I own it. I made it. I set up a fake school list. I set up a death list. A list that's for all the people I thought needed to be taught a lesson. And, of course, I added myself to throw off suspicion." I laughed at the memory. "You thought me being on that list was so funny."

I kept moving. "So I had Maybelle as my first victim. She was such an easy lay. So quick to please a boy, and Steve Biselle was that boy. I followed her after choir practice, snuck up behind her, and hit her over the head." I paused. "God that felt so good. Anyway, Dad helped me move the body to the woods, and I cut off her clothes and stabbed her. Gave her exactly what she deserved."

Mike was horrified now, looking from me to my parents and back.

"Oh, didn't you know my dad was a serial killer back in his day?" I laughed. "It runs in the family. The good old genes. The serial killer slash forensic scientist teaching his offspring his ways." I turned back to Mike. "Now. *That* is the answer to your other question. Why were the murders only committed on a Monday night? Because it's the only night when dear old Dad is home from work and can help me out. Plus it helps him keep up his skills. So, that's why it only happened on Mondays, because I had help. And that's why Steve had to go, because he had absolutely no trouble taking advantage of poor little Maybelle and bragging about it to his friends. And..." I waved my hand around. "It took him only two days to hit on Janelle after poor little Maybelle was dead. Talk about *no morals*." I paused. "That's also why Janelle had to go, and the jocks were just an added bonus."

I picked up the photos of their crime scene. "See. It was easy for me to kill the girls, but I needed help with the guys. They're bigger than me, so dear old

Dad comes in handy for moving dead bodies." I threw the pictures into the bin. "How I loved the feel and smell and taste of Maybelle and Janelle's naked bodies under mine." I picked up a box of matches and lit one, watching it burn brightly, and after flicking it into the bin, I watched naked bodies burn. "Don't worry, Mikey. If you think the smoke alarm will go off and bring help, not only is it turned off, but the whole room is fire proof." His expression still said horrified.

"Janelle was no better than Maybelle. Hiking up her skirt, giving head to the jocks." I shook my head. "Those girls just have absolutely no morals. The boys called each other studs to each other's faces, but called the girls sluts behind their backs. All while they were getting blow jobs and quick fucks." I threw more papers into the flames.

"You asked the questions, Mikey. You figured it out. I added anyone I wanted to the death list. I changed notes and comments to suit myself at will. I made the site, I made the rules."

"But Kristen and Mr Smooth weren't on that list," Mike managed through his quiet sobs.

"No," I said, thinking. "That happened rather quickly. I only noticed it happening on the Thursday and Friday. Saw them having sex in the tech cupboard on Monday, and decided to do something about it that night." I pulled the crossbow from under the cupboard. "I thought I'd get creative with that one. And when I saw them against the tree, a teacher having sex with a student, I fired. The camera was on a tripod every time, unless I moved toward the body. And I was careful never to be seen. Only my gloved hand was seen in Maybelle's video, nothing else. With Kristen and Dick, I just cut their clothes off and used Dick's blood to write on his back. Their deaths were rather unplanned." I stood in front of him. "Just like yours will be."

CHAPTER TEN

Tuesday morning I rode the bus to school alone. I walked into the gym alone. I walked into class alone. Mrs Mendoza asked me if I knew where Mike was. I told her I didn't, and then went into the hallway with the police officer who questioned me about Mike's disappearance.

His body had been found in the heavy dense forest behind his house by their dog, Chuckles. He'd been laid out on a bed of weeds, fully clothed, a single hole in his chest.

My chest ached as I recalled the previous night. It was horrifying that I had to do that to my best friend, but he had figured out too much and had to go.

Once we'd left his body, I spent the rest of the night deleting www.badluck-youredead.com in between bouts of guilty tears and pain. There was no way I was going to post Mikey's video to the net, or any photos to social media. Besides, I had no social media accounts, and I'd used enough professional software to create the website that there was no way anyone could connect it to me. The gift of being a computer whiz and the son of a serial killer forensic scientist.

I knew the funerals for Mikey, Janelle and the jocks, Kristen and Dick were coming up. Anyone would be able to attend, regardless of the horrifying knowledge that a teacher had been having a sexual relationship with an underage student.

I spent recess and lunch alone, thinking about everything I'd done and how done I felt. No Mikey to play sport with. No Mikey to tease and torment. No Mikey…

I didn't even take notice of the lessons in the afternoon and just sat staring out the window. I guess my teachers felt sorry for me and let it pass.

Now, I rode the bus home alone. Alone. As much as I craved the attention of a best friend, I also knew that if I wanted to follow in my parents' footsteps then alone is what I needed to be. I descended the bus steps and breathed in the air. If I wanted to be a *serial killer* then alone is what I needed to be.

Of course, I could also be a computer whiz, a top notch scientist, or a lawyer.

But no. This life chose me, and it's what I want to be. So alone it has to be.

THE BONES OF WRATH:
CHANGES

PROPHETICUS MOTHIMUS

My eyes slowly drifted closed and then struggled to rise again. I lazily took in the dark depths of my bedroom. It was dark because it was close to midnight, and the depths were because of the shadows being cast around the room due to the street light flashing long streaks of orange and yellow around my curtain edges.

My eyes drifted closed again, but I forced them open. I couldn't move. My body was so comfortable in my soft cosy bed. My muscles were lazy, unable to move, to work, to do anything. But then, I didn't want to do anything.

I was so tired. Not just the normal tired of being at school all day, soccer practice, homework, and so on, but tired in every way; physically, emotionally, mentally. I think that kind of tired is called *exhausted,* and I was feeling it. Badly!

I had full days, so it didn't help that every night for the past week I had been constantly woken by a flapping sound. Yet every morning when I told my parents, they couldn't find anything. No bird, no bug, no fly. Nothing.

There was nothing there. I felt my eyelids descend for the last time. I wanted to fight it, I did, but I just didn't…have…the…strength…

F. F. F. F. F. F. F…

What, what…mmm…what was that? I buried my head into the pillow.

Fl. Fl. Fl. Fl. Fl. Fl. Fl…

"Mmmm…" It sounded as if it was right beside my ear, flapping away.

It was back!

I manically brushed empty air beside my ear and scrambled out of bed, flicking the lamp on beside me, and spinning around to see what it was all in one fluid motion.

I frantically looked everywhere, corners, floor, ceiling, ceiling, ceiling…there it was…

Fla. Fla. Fla. Fla. Fla. Fla…

Flapping away in the corner of the ceiling was a moth.

"A moth!" I was so disappointed at this mundane revelation that I stood staring at it while it slowly settled down and sat silently staring back at me.

Yes. That's what it was doing. Staring back at me. Even though it looked like a small common house moth, I had the weird feeling it was staring back at me, studying me, the way I was studying it.

I shivered and shook my head. That's not possible. I looked around for something to swat it with and picked up an old t-shirt. Bunching up the bottom in my hand so it was a long bat-like structure,

I slowly moved over to the corner, lifted my arm up behind me, and when I was close enough, lashed out and slapped him off the wall.

He fell like a petal, fluttering to the floor.

I watched him as he lay there, on his back, legs and wings flapping…slowly…then he stopped. I quickly grabbed an ugly bowl I had made in ceramics class the day before from my desk and put it over him.

"There, no more flapping." I'd get Mum or Dad to get rid of him tomorrow. I slid back into bed, straightened the covers and turned off the light.

*****

"Did you get rid of that moth that's been bothering me?" I climbed into the back seat of our minivan after school and dumped my bag on the floor.

"What moth?" Mum asked as my brother slammed the sliding door. "There *was* no moth."

"The moth I told you about this morning." I buckled myself in and settled back. "I told you he was under that ugly bowl on the floor, and he's probably the one who's been waking me up every night for the last week."

Mum pulled into the lane and my brother piped up beside me. "Oooh, Davey's been scared of a moth, ooohhh ooohhh." He was lightly throwing his basketball in the air.

He may be three years older than me, but he can act three years younger sometimes.

"What do you *mean* there was no moth? I swatted him last night." I leaned forward to look at Mum in the rear-view. "He was *definitely* there."

"He may have been last night, but he wasn't this morning." She turned left at the main road instead of right. "We're doing some shopping before we go home."

Bert and I groaned and pulled faces at each other.

"Now stop that. Behave and you can have tacos tonight."

"Yay, tacos," we cheered, the moth suddenly forgotten at the mention of food.

*****

I thoroughly examined my room when I got home and again before I got into bed. Window locked tight, no moths on the floor, or in corners, or behind curtains, or even under the clothes dumped in piles on the floor. Nothing! Zip, zilch, nada!

Frustrated as to where it could have gone and to even *how* it could have gotten out from under the bowl, which was quite heavy; I got into bed and put my hands behind my head. *At least I know it's a moth. It's just a moth.* I snuggled down into my cosy, soft bed. *It's just…a…moth…*

F. F. F. F. F. F. F…

"Mmm, what…?" I drifted in and out.

Fl. Fl. Fl. Fl. Fl. Fl. Fl…

I frowned and breathed deeply. Not again!!!

Fla. Fla. Fla. Fla. Fla. Fla. Fla…

My hand snaked out from under the covers and over to the bedside cupboard. Flicking on the lamp, I peeked out to see where it was.

Back in the same corner it was last night.

I sat up and looked. *That's not the same moth! This one's bigger.* I crawled out of bed and grabbed my t-shirt again. Creeping over to the corner, I looked. Yep, definitely bigger. Last night's had been about the size of a ten cent piece. This one looked to be about the size of fifty-cents.

"Well," I muttered. "Either it grew, or I've got moths!" I raised my arm and swung my shirt, knocking the moth to the floor. I grabbed the ceramic bowl and covered him, then grabbed one of my encyclopaedias and placed that on top. "There, you won't get out now." I went back to bed and fell asleep.

After waking with the sun, I got up, dressed, and stumbled over to the book on the floor. I grabbed it, and got ready to hit the moth with it when I lifted the bowl. Slowly…slowly…and…I… Gotchya—

My hand paused in mid-air.

The moth was gone.

Huh? A few moments later, I was digging around in the laundry and dropped a can of carpet cleaner in my search for moth killing juice.

"What are you doing?" Mum called from the kitchen.

"Looking for the fly spray," I called back, picking up the can and placing it back on the shelf before walking down the hall to my room.

"What do you need that for?" Mum asked as I passed.

"To kill the moth that's been bugging me." I walked into my room, took aim and fired. I sprayed in every corner, under the bed, in the closet, around the window, behind cupboards, under my desk. I even picked my clothes up from the floor. I made sure my door was closed tight before leaving. If it was there it would die before I got home from school.

*****

Except it didn't, because apparently there was nothing in my room to die. I dragged the vacuum cleaner down the hall, plugged it in, and started cleaning behind cupboards, under my bed, my desk, around the windows. I saw my brother standing in the doorway leaning casually against the doorjamb with his basketball in hand.

"Dude, what *are* you doing?" He flipped the ball from hand to hand, staring at me in amazement. "You *never* do housework."

"I'm not now." I turned it off. "Just trying to get rid of an annoying moth that's been bugging me at night." I dragged the vacuum past him and back into the laundry.

I got into bed knowing it wouldn't be back, and silently, and mentally, high-fived myself. I shouldn't have been so quick to congratulate…

F. F. F. F. F. F. F…

Ugh, that flapping sound's back.

Fl. Fl. Fl. Fl. Fl. Fl. Fl…

I dragged myself out of a deep sleep, out of bed, and turned the bedside light on. Looking around, I saw it…but…it…couldn't…be…

I stared.

That can't be the same moth? That one was small; this one's the size of my whole hand.

It…was…huge!!!

I stared in horror and gulped.

Fla. Fla. Fla. Fla. Fla. Fla…

Its wings seemed to beat in slow motion while the greenish circles on them glittered in the light with every movement.

That can't be the same…

Horrified by the sight, but not taking my eyes off it, I crept to the door, opened it, and closed it behind me, then headed down the hall for the laundry. I grabbed the fly spray, sneaked back to my room and silently entered. The moth was still there, settled in the same corner as the others had been. I tiptoed over, lifted my hand, and sprayed.

Flap Flap Flap Flap Flap Flap Flap.

The moth went wild, slapping itself against one wall then the other, then back again, all while staying in the same corner of the room.

I stepped back to watch, choking on the repellents' spray. The moth slowed, its wings spread wide, struggling to cope under the fumes. Slower, slower, it slowly slapped its wings down the wall and onto the carpet.

I moved closer and peered down at it. Legs moved…wings fluttered. I placed my ceramic bowl over it and went back to bed, trying not to choke on the spray.

*****

The next morning I asked my friends if they'd ever seen one so big. We were in the school library and I was looking for books on moths.

"Yeah, man," Ned said, spreading his arms wide. "It was huge. Ate my whole head." The others guffawed and slapped him on the back.

"It's true." Ned brushed the hands away. "It was *huge*."

I pulled another book off the shelf and flicked through it. "Well, I don't know if it's the same one or I've got an infestation. It's gotten way bigger every night."

"It will eat your head soon," Ned piped up, grabbing a book.

"What are you so worried about, Davey?" Mike asked over my shoulder. "Just get your parents to deal with it."

"I did, but each time they said it wasn't there." I put the book back and glanced over the spines of the ones next to it. "That's all they have. I didn't find it anywhere."

"Maybe you should ask the librarian. They have reference books on moths," Mike added. "Or you could try Google."

We all looked at each other and headed for the computer bank.

"No running." The middle-aged librarian gave us her sternest look.

We reddened and apologised while typing moths + grows fast + circles on wings. I hit search and waited. I glanced at the images that popped up on screen, eagerly searching for the one in my room. "That's it," I cried, clicking on the image.

It looked exactly like the moth I'd been seeing every night. It was a brownish grey colour with iridescent circles on its wings.

"The Propheticus Mothimus," Andrew read over my shoulder. "Click on it so we can read about it."

I clicked on the image and the website popped up. "*Spells, Tells, and Tall Tales True,*" I read as the bell rang.

"Time to go," the librarian called. "Next class is up."

I panicked and quickly hit the print button. "We'll have to read it later," I told the others as we waited for the pages to print.

"Boys, you need to leave now." She came over in our direction.

"Just printing something, Miss," I said. "It seems to be quite long." I watched page number six print out.

"Well, the others can wait for you outside. Move along boys."

They gave me apologetic stares and moved off. "I'll be out in a minute," I called and quickly checked the pop-up window. "One more," I told the librarian. Fifteen seconds later I grabbed the pile of paper, shoved it into my bag, and left.

*****

I sat at my desk flicking my pen. I'd been there for two hours finishing up homework and reading, and I still had another page to go. Leaning back in my chair, I groaned at the pain in my back. "Man, that's what I get for bending over for two hours." I flung my arms above my head, hoping to stretch out the aches and pain, then picked up my book. "Blah, blah, blah. Blah, blah, blah!"

I slammed it shut, piled up my books, and shoved them into my bag for the next day. One piece of paper in a folder creased up and I pulled it out. "Hey, it's the stuff from the library." I pulled out the rest and…started…reading…

F. F. F. F. F. F. F…

Mmm… I moved my head slightly, wondering why my neck hurt.

Fl. Fl. Fl. Fl. Fl. Fl. Fl…

"Go away," I mumbled, snuggling my head into my bed. Why's it so hard? I forced myself to wake, my lids slowly rising to the occasion. The reason my bed was so hard is that it wasn't my bed at all. I was looking at the floor in my bedroom because I'd fallen asleep at my desk.

Fla. Fla. Fla. Fla. Fla. Fla. Fla…

No, no, it cannot possibly be back. No.

I squeezed my eyes tight, willing it to go away.

Silence.

Had it read my mind and gone away? I felt the hairs rise on the back of my neck.

"Davey..." whispered ever so quietly through my room.

My eyes flew open. "Mum? Dad?"

"Davey..."

Sweat dripped down my brow, across my arm, and onto my desk making my forehead and arm slick. Sweat slid down my chilly, shivering spine into my pants.

"Davey..."

I gulped, squeezed my eyes closed, open and closed again...

"Davey..."

Ever so slowly, I turned my head to the side. My desk was facing the window; the door was to my back and my bed to my left. I saw the bed. I saw the wall with its posters beside it. I looked all the way up to the ceiling...

Nothing!

"Davey...I'm here for you..."

Clenching my jaw in fear, I let my gaze slowly move along the ceiling to the wall behind me. The view was partially hidden by my left shoulder, so I peeked over it. Gently flapping in the corner of the room was the moth.

It was now the size of my head!!!

My head lifted in fear, and then my shoulder and torso moved up until I was standing facing it.

It. Was. The size. Of. My. Head!

"Davey…I am here for you…" Its wingspan was so great now they could flap against the wall on either side of the corner.

My head started moving from side to side. *No, no, this cannot be happening. Not happening. No!* I dived under my covers and turned off the light. I squeezed everything tight. My eyes, my muscles, my arms and legs around me, all locked into a ball as small as I could be, and wrapped the covers around me until I couldn't breathe.

F. F. F. F. F. F. F…

"Go away," I yelled, dragging the covers back to uncover my mouth.

Fl. Fl. Fl. Fl. Fl. Fl. Fl…

"Davey…I am here for you…Davey."

"No. No, you are not. You are extinct and a figment of my imagination. You do not exist. *Not. Exist!*" My muscles shook violently from being squeezed to death, and I was sweating profusely. Even more than I did when I played soccer.

"Davey…I am here for you…it is your destiny… it is time…"

"No. No, not possible. Not happening. Go Away." I shivered, and I'm not sure how long after, but I no longer heard flapping. I freed my head and turned on the light. Nothing. With a sigh of relief I settled back and threw the covers off. Panting, I waited until my body cooled down and my breathing was back to normal before turning to turn off the bedside lamp.

"Argh." I threw myself back against the wall as

flat as I could and gazed at the face of the moth that now sat on my desk.

Yes, I said a moth was sitting on my desk. And did I also say…face?

It didn't really have *a* face. Not like a *human* face, but I… I grasped the covers around me, pushing myself into the wall in fear, for it had grown.

Yes, *grown*.

It was no longer the size of my head, but at least half the size of…*me*. My *body*.

It gazed upon me, wings folded across its back. "It is your destiny Davey…there is no need to be afraid." Something you could call a mouth moved while it spoke.

Fl. Fl. Fl. Fl. Fl. Fl. Fl…up it rose, the soft humming of its wings sending papers flying across the room.

"Arggghhhhhh…" I dived under the covers.

*****

"Davey…? Davey…?" Mum flung the bed covers back to find me in a wet puddle of sweat. "Oh, my God, Davey. What's wrong?" Her hand went to my forehead. "You're burning up. We need to get you into the shower. Come on." Half dragging, half carrying me, she got me into the bathroom, pushed me into the shower, and turned it on.

"Ah, ah." My teeth chattered. "That's cold." I hugged myself to keep from freezing.

Mum popped a stool into the cubicle. "Sit for a

bit. You're boiling and we need to keep you cool. I'll go and strip your bed."

I sat shivering under the cold fast spray and only half-heartedly washed myself. I mean, I still had my clothes on, so what was the point in washing myself? My eyelids felt like the Sahara Desert was in them, and my bones and muscles ached like I'd never felt before. I was sick, and nearly vomited, but nothing came out.

"Okay, let's check your temperature." Mum flung back the door and stuck the thermometer into my ear. "Okay, not so hot now. I've got you clean clothes, so dry off and change into those. Then you can lie on the couch while your bed dries out. It was soaked."

After she left, I turned off the taps and struggled out of the shower. I felt horrible, and it took all of my strength to pull off my night clothes, dry off, and dress in the dry pjs Mum had left. I looked at myself in the mirror. Ugh, God! What was happening to me? My skin was ash grey, my hair no longer the brown it used to be.

Am I dying? Do I have a disease? Why do I look so horrible?

I tried to lick my lips, but my tongue was like sandpaper and felt fat and numb. I shuffled into the kitchen where I grabbed a bottle of juice, and shuffled to the lounge room to flake out on the couch for the rest of the day.

*****

I wasn't feeling much better when Dad tucked me into bed that night. "Don't worry, Davey. This will all be over tomorrow."

"Her ther er ner?" I mumbled around my fat tongue.

He smiled knowingly. "Because I went through the same thing at your age. It runs in the family. Me, my father, his father, and his before him. It will be over soon." He kissed me goodnight and walked out the door.

I drifted in and out of sleep feeling feverish and achy.

What is happening? What is going on? Why do I hurt? Why am I having nightmares about moths? This is not real. Not real…not real…

F. F. F. F. F. F. F…

No. No it is not real. No.

"Davey…it is time…Davey."

No. You do not exist; you are just a figment of my imagination. My very feverish, sick imagination.

Fl. Fl. Fl. Fl. Fl. Fl. Fl…

"Davey…it is time…"

"No." My eyelids struggled to open. "No," I repeated.

"Come with me, Davey…"

I felt a cool breeze on my face and opened my eyes to see the moth flapping above me. Bigger. The size *of* me, my *bed,* my *room.* It looked down at me, its mouth and eyes visible and clear. "Come with me, Davey…it is time…"

My eyes widened. "No," I yelled. "Mum, Dad." I buried myself under the covers.

"Davey, what is it?" Mum came running into the room.

"Make it go away. It's here, it's here," I yelled.

"What's here? There's nothing here, Davey."

I peeked out from the covers to find my parents standing over me, the light casting a halo around them as they stood there in their pyjamas looking down at me with strange expressions on their faces.

"The moth, it was here. It was the size of my bed."

"It's okay, Davey, it's okay." Mum sat beside me. "There's nothing to fear about this. It's just part of your initiation into adulthood."

My fuzzied brain tried to keep up. "Initiation? Adulthood? For what?"

"Yes, Davey. This is what happens when the males of the family turn twelve. You start to change." She patted my shoulder. "There's nothing to fear. It will all be over in a month, you'll be back at school in no time, and you won't remember a thing. Until you become a father that is. Just let your father do what he needs to."

I looked at Dad who was standing beside her. "Dad? What does she mean?"

"It will only hurt a little bit for a short time, but it will be over quickly," he added as large wings burst out of his back and his arms and hands receded. He floated into the air with the same flapping sound I'd heard for a week. "Davey…" the moth hissed. "It is time."

Dad? No…Dad?!

He flapped above me, wings going faster and faster creating a cool fast wind that made my curtains and bedwear billow, while Mum quickly retreated to the door.

"It will all be over soon, Davey," she said, grasping the doorjamb for support. Physical or emotional? I couldn't tell.

"No…no…" My head shook as much as the rest of me.

Flap. Flap. Flap. Flap. Flap. Flap. Flap…

The bed covers flew off revealing my shaking weak body.

"No…no…"

What is going on, what is happening? Why is Dad a moth? This cannot be happening. It cannot be…what is…

"It is time, Davey. Do not be afraid."

He was the size of *me*, my *bed*, my *room*.

"No. No."

He hovered over me, wings thrashing faster and faster so he could hover closer and closer, as close as he could without losing momentum.

"No…nooo," I yelled as he settled over me and my bed. "Nooooo." His moth-like arms and his moth-like lips grabbed me, holding me, imprisoning me. I thrashed around with what little strength I had left. "Nooooo."

His face came down on mine…

He ate me whole…

*****

"Hey, Mum, where did Dad an' Davey go?" Bert

asked, standing in the doorway of his brother's room and wondering where they'd both disappeared to so suddenly in the middle of the night. And why.

"They'll be back in a month or so." She passed him in the hallway. "Davey needs treatment because he's not well, so your father's looking after him and has taken him to see some specialists interstate."

Bert wandered into Davey's room, gently throwing the ball from hand to hand. Spying some paper under the bed, he bent down and picked it up before sitting on the bed to read it.

"The Propheticus Mothimus is an extinct half-moth half-human hybrid creature that comes from the jungles of Tanzanite in South Baribbia. It was originally said the moth part of the hybrid was only ever seen when someone from the long line of shaman was sick or about to die. But while the old human body died, the soul did not, taking on the form of the moth in its newly created human body, confined to change into the form forever and passing the genetic malformation down to his human/moth male descendants. The change happens when the human heir turns twelve…"

ALIEN MASTER COOK

"Welcome to the Trifest Children's Master Cook Masterclass Cooking Competition!" The woman in the white chef's outfit called across the vast room filled with benches of food and cooking equipment. "This is the first class of its kind." She clapped her hands to silence the excited crowd of children. "We will start with round one. You all have numbers on your shirts. They correspond with the numbers on the benches. Match your shirt number to a bench. This will be your bench for today's first heat." She spread her arms wide and we all stood transfixed. "You will be whipping up an entrée, main and dessert. Those who get through the first heat will go on to the second, and so on and so forth until we have the winner of the *Trifest Children's Master Cook Masterclass Cooking Competition.*"

One hundred ten-to-fifteen-year-olds cheered, me included. I was number 88, two fat ladies if you played bingo. My friend Jennifer was number 11, legs eleven. And no, while this wasn't bingo, we do volunteer at the local rec centre which holds bingo classes on weekends. It sucked that we were so far apart in the huge expansive space. I think it was an airport hangar, or at least it was once upon a time, as we certainly weren't at an airport now.

Jennifer grabbed my arm. "I hope we get through all the heats; it will be so cool."

I smiled excitedly, mirroring her expression. "Me too."

"Children, to your benches." The woman talking was Grand Master Cook, Dionne Warren. She'd been in the business for almost fifty years and had gone from an apprentice in London to owner of fifteen restaurants, a book author, TV show host, videos, you name it; she had it, including her face on the aprons we were wearing. The cooking comp had been her idea in the next step to her expanding empire, and Jen and I hoped to be the winners.

At thirteen we'd been best friends since forever and started cooking at six. Well, mixing and licking the spoon anyway.

I took my place near the back of the room. At ten benches per row, I was third from the back, and it felt a little isolated.

Jen was in the second row and so far away. I nervously glanced at everything. Lights, cameras, people running everywhere. It was being filmed for TV, and my stomach was full of butterflies. I smoothed down my apron as Dionne spoke again.

"In front of you is a piece of paper. On the paper is a set of recipes to choose from for the entrée you will be making. If you look to the right and left of the room, you will see fridges and racks of vegetables. You have your staple ingredients under your benches."

I glanced down to see oils, butter, salt, pepper and a small variety of other things.

"You will have thirty minutes to create a delicious mouth-watering starter to an amazing meal. We want something quick and simple to make at home, and want to see what your skills and abilities are. We will give you a minute to decide which recipe to choose, and then you will hear the siren. Are you ready Master Cooks?"

"Yes."

"What did you say?"

"Yes."

"I said, are you ready Master Cooks?"

"Yes, Chef!" one hundred children yelled out.

"Good. You have one minute from now to pick from the list…and…go."

I scanned the recipe list in front of me, wondering if I knew how to make any of them. There was at least one hundred, enough for one per kid I suppose, but then I doubted we'd all pick a different recipe. I counted on one hand how many I actually knew how to do, and quickly worked out which would be the best. Prawn cocktail.

Yeah, I know. Simple and plain and boring to some, but not the way I did it.

Blaaaaaaaaaaaaarrrrrrrrrrrrr…

Many of us covered our ears as the horn sounded, and when it was over, we ran in an excited daze to the fridges and racks. I gathered my ingredients and raced for my bench, immediately putting a frypan on the stove and slow heating a dob of butter in it. While that melted, I de-veined my king prawns and sliced them in half long ways before whipping up a quick batter. I dunked the prawns in it, then lightly slid them into the pan to crisp up. After chopping some red cabbage, celery, parsley, carrot, apple and craisins, I turned my prawns and mixed oil, garlic and chive together for the salad. I turned off the prawns just as I heard…

"Time to plate up."

I tossed the salad and put a handful into the martini glass I'd grabbed from the shelf, crunched some nuts on, added my vinegar, and gently laid the prawns decoratively on top.

"Time is up. Step away from your benches."

I grabbed my towel, wiped my hands, and rubbed the back of my hand across my forehead. I was sweating and noticed how warm it was in the hangar.

"We will now come around and taste them all." Adults in chef uniforms descended on us from the side.

It looks like Dionne won't be tasting them herself, I thought. *Understandable since there's so many of us.*

Her assistants chewed through the aisles with hands grabbing food and shoving it into mouths.

Gosh, they're hungry, I thought, watching as food was devoured from the outside in.

When an assistant got to me and inhaled a piece of prawn with some salad, her eyes widened, almost unnaturally so, and slowly turned to the left as she looked at me. It was creepy, I gotta say, and I stepped back again. Her arm went up and waved someone over.

Dionne appeared by her side, as if by magic, and she pointed to my meal.

Silently, Dionne dipped a prawn into the salad and put it to her mouth. She sniffed deeply with flared nostrils, looked enquiringly at it with a cocked brow, and then opened her mouth wide. Huge teeth chomped down on half the prawn, and after a few movements, her mouth inhaled the second half. Her eyes widened. Her brows went up to her hairline. Her face went a little red, a little sweaty, a little…surprised…

"Um," I muttered, scared I had poisoned the world's most famous chef. "Is it all right?" I twisted the towel in my hand.

"All right," she boomed. "It's more than all right. It's downright delicious. You are through to the second heat of the *Trifest Children's Master Cook Masterclass Cooking Competition.*"

My eyes widened, and I felt the jealous stares of those around me. "What? What do you mean I'm through? I only did an entrée. I thought we had to do all three?"

"Not today. I have changed the rules," Dionne roared as she turned around. "If your recipe is perfect, we will pick you straight away, otherwise you'll have to wait until the end of the day." She turned back to me. "But you, number 88, are through. One of my assistants will show you to the waiting area where you'll stay for the rest of today. Good luck."

She walked away as an assistant beckoned me to follow her. I felt daggers in my back as I walked out of the hangar into a huge waiting area.

"There is food and drink plus a TV to watch. Feel free to change the channel." She walked out and left me there.

I couldn't hear anything happening, so settled in to watch TV. I was munching on a sandwich two hours later when two more contestants walked in. Neither was Jennifer. "Hi."

"Hi," they replied.

"You got chosen to go through to the next heat with your mains?" I gulped back a mouthful of Pepsi Max.

"Yep," said number 2, grabbing a can of drink and sculling it back. "Gosh, I'm so thirsty." He burped and went red when he saw our faces. "Sorry. I'm Ken."

"Darcy," I replied. "Help yourself to anything. We've only got TV to watch."

Number 23 finished off a triple-decker ham, cheese and tomato sandwich. "I'm so hungry," she managed around her food. "I'm Michelle."

"Dionne loved your mains?"

"Yep," they replied together.

We settled in, and two hours later three more

contestants came in.

"Darcy," Jennifer yelled as we ran for each other and jumped up and down, squealing.

"You made it, yay." I was so glad my bestie was going through to the next heat with me. "What did you get through with?"

"My raspberry chiffon pie." She took the can of drink I gave her and cracked it open.

"With the special ingredient?" I had eaten Jen's amazing pie before, many times, and always wondered what the special ingredient was. But she never told me.

She swallowed. "Yup! I think that's what Dionne picked up on and she told me she'd never tasted that in a pie before." She took a bite of sandwich.

"What was your special ingredient?" a girl with number 93 on her apron asked.

Jennifer laughed. "I can't give that away in a cooking comp, I'd be nuts."

An assistant came in. "Those who didn't pass have gone home and the rest are waiting, so come out, and Dionne will tell you about tomorrow."

We followed her into the main hangar and crowded around the front benches.

"Children." Dionne waved her arms for silence. Jennifer and I excitedly clung to each other. "You have made it into the second heat of the *Trifest Children's Master Cook Masterclass Cooking Competition*. Congratulations. Go home. We will see you tomorrow for an even harder round than today."

*****

The next day we did it all again, except this time there were fifty of us. We had new numbers and clean aprons, and were starting from the beginning. I was 42 and Jen was 5.

"All right, children." Dionne stood at the front once more. "This time the recipes are a little harder. We want to test you to see what your capabilities are, and just because you got through yesterday, does not mean you will get through today. Once again you have one minute to pick a recipe from the list in front of you and then you'll start. Give us different, give us unusual…give us…" She looked into the air for the answer. "Out of this world amazing. Now pick your recipe."

I read through a list of entrées I could choose from, but this time there was only fifty, and this time they were a little out of my league. I'd done only three of them to what I considered perfection, and it might be harder to pull off.

Blaaaaaaaaaaaaarrrrrrrrrrrrr.

The siren sounded and we were off.

I grabbed my ingredients and raced back to my bench with bacon, chicken, beans, pineapple and onions. I heated the pan with butter and threw crushed garlic and diced onion into the frypan. I chopped the chicken into strips, and cut the fat off the bacon slices before frying them and laying them on a plate while I cooked the beans and pineapple slices in the pan. I rolled up three strips of chicken in a strip of bacon and started plating up.

I laid the pineapple down first, topped it off with bacon rolled chicken, and placed the beans artistically on top before drizzling the remaining mixture over it and around the plate.

Blaaaaaaaaaaaaarrrrrrrrrrrrr.

I nearly dropped the pan at the sound of the bell and took a step back to recover. After putting the pan on the stove I grabbed my towel, and a moment later the assistants descended again. Half an hour later five contestants had been sent to the waiting room and I wasn't one of them.

"Bugger," I mumbled with a sigh.

Our bench tops were cleaned down, something I didn't know about yesterday due to going through so quickly, and we got ready to start lunch.

"Children, we are about to start our main course. You have one hour to prepare and plate a meal worthy of remembering. Please read your recipe list and make a choice. You have one minute."

I decided to stick with my chicken theme and picked a recipe I could give a new taste to. Collecting the food, I got to work.

I butterflied a chicken breast, then mixed up my special ingredient marinade and smeared it all over. After heating the grill, I quickly whipped up special cheese dough to make a bread roll and shoved it into the oven so I could slow grill a capsicum and strips of cucumber. I made a spread of cheese and chive butter, cut some pineapple slices, and waited for the bread. I slow grilled the chicken, removed the other stuff, and sliced through my now baked bread roll, smearing on the special butter. I cut up the chicken and laid some slices across the bottom of the bun, topped it off with the other ingredients, and placed the top of the bun on an angle just as the siren rang.

Standing back, I watched everyone else. Some hadn't finished, and one was waving away smoke after burning the food. I craned my neck to see Jen, and she turned around and waved, giving me a thumbs up to let me know she had finished on time.

The assistant eyed my burger, put the top on, and placed it in her mouth. Her eyes slid closed, in delight I hoped, and she waved over Dionne who licked her lips in anticipation.

Wait…was her tongue green…?

She must have eaten something to change its colour, I thought before realizing she'd swallowed the rest of my burger.

Her eyes widened and glassed over. Her head cocked to the side. Her tongue slid out and over her lips. It was long…and green.

Wait…was her tongue…forked…?

No, I must be imagining things. Maybe I need something to eat.

"Congratulations number 42, you are through to the third heat of the *Trifest Children's Master Cook Masterclass Cooking Competition.*"

"Yay," Jennifer squealed from two rows away.

I gave her the thumbs up and walked to the waiting room.

*****

On day three, we were down to twenty-five contestants with Jennifer and me as two of them. She'd won again with her dessert, and now we were numbers 9 and 23. This time I made it through to the dessert round without leaving until Dionne tried my pineapple upside down cake. And this time, several assistants crowded around all downing pieces of it.

"Mmmmm, mmm," was all I heard as twenty-five contestants stared at them gobbling down my dessert. Hands reached for more and shovelled into mouths. Mouths that now seemed bigger, fingers now seemed longer, and tongues all licked lips. Forked tongues.

"No." I shook my head. "I must need to eat, have low blood sugar or something. I cannot be seeing forked tongues."

"Congratulations number 23, you are through to heat 4 of the *Trifest Children's Master Cook Masterclass Cooking Competition*," Dionne called out. "You are a *very* good cook." She and her assistant looked at me, licking their lips with long green tongues.

"Ummm." I gulped. "Thanks." I quickly ran to the waiting room and waited for Jennifer who came to my place after it was over.

"Have you noticed how they are around food?" I threw myself onto my bed and pulled a pillow under my chin. "They must really love their food, but they get this really weird look on their faces when they eat."

"What do you mean?" Jennifer was flipping through the clothes in my wardrobe. "Where's that new coat you got? I want to see it."

"It's the blue and pink one. Haven't you noticed their eyes go wide and kinda glaze over, and everything else gets kinda big too? Their mouths, their fingers, and their tongues seem green. Unless they ate something today to make them that colour." I sat up as Jen pulled my new coat from the closet and tried it on. "Did you notice their tongues were green, and I could swear they were forked as well?" I watched her parade back and forth. "Green forked tongues. I could not have imagined that, Jen? Help me out here. Tell me you saw something."

"Did you eat between cooking?" Jen looked in the floor length mirror. "You know you go a bit wacko when you don't eat, and you *do* have an overactive imagination." She turned left then right, eyeing my jacket from every angle. "I have got to get me one of these."

"Yes, smarty pants, I did eat. But it did get quite warm in there, maybe I just got caught up in it. Maybe I..." I sighed. "I dunno. I could swear I saw forked tongues."

Jennifer pulled out some of my hats to match the jacket. "I didn't notice anything except for how into your cake they were." She turned to me, a thoughtful look on her face. "It was like a feeding frenzy, so it was a bit weird." She turned back to the mirror. "We're down to the final twelve, so we'll keep an eye out tomorrow."

*****

Day four, heat four, and we were down to twelve contestants. Today I was number 12 and Jennifer number 1. We were four rows away from each other. It might as well be opposite ends of the world, because that's what it seemed like.

At the front of the room, Dionne slicked her dark brown hair back and clapped her hands. "This is it. Today we narrow the field down to two. That means ten of you will be going home by the end of the day."

Jennifer glanced around and flashed a quick smile.

God, I was nervous. Not only was I in the last heat for the *Trifest Children's Master Cook Cooking Comp*, but I was being closely watched by assistants at the side of the room.

Are their eyes bigger? Why are they watching me so weirdly? I felt butterflies belt around my insides and noticed one assistant lick her lips. *Nope. It was pink and normal today. Mmm...well that's—*

"Pick your recipe for your entrée and get started."

I glanced down at twelve entrée names I'd never heard of.

"You'll notice that these are unusual recipes. Ones you may have never heard of. They are from many foreign countries, small out of the way places you won't even find on a map, whose people eat these delicacies on a regular basis. That's why we have supplied the full recipe for them. Today you get to make food you've never made before, to broaden your horizons into other cultures. Please… collect your ingredients."

I gulped. The recipes sounded horrendous, and there was one with eel and something called Bug Choi. I wandered over to the fridge and collected the ingredients. Slowly following the recipe, I sautéed garlic, chilli, and chive into a frypan full of butter, and added chopped onion and cabbage. In another pan, I slowly cooked off strips of eel (blech) and black pellet type things I assumed was the Bug Choi. After dishing up some fried salad in a bowl, I was turning the eel over in the pan when one of the black pellets jumped

"Whoa." I jumped too and watched in amazement as all three started bouncing around. "What the, hey—" I saw one explode open and legs popped out. "Hey, what the?" Everyone turned and stared in shock as a second black pellet exploded open and landed on its back in the pan with multiple legs all waving around.

"Do not worry." Dionne came swanning over. "These bugs are a delicacy."

"Bugs!?" My eyes bulged open. "Real bugs? I'm cooking real bugs?" I stared in horror at the frypan. "I'm cooking real bugs?" I watched the third one explode open and land on what I presumed, was its stomach.

Dionne smacked each one hard on the back with a mallet. "Yes. Bug Choi are bugs that come alive when cooked, but you simply hit them and they die.

As I said, they are a delicacy, and many people in their country love them." She flattened them out. "There. They are cooked now. Plate up everybody."

I felt sick and wanted to vomit, but held it together to use tongs to put the eel and bugs on the plate with the fried salad. "Ugh!" I threw the tongs in the bin and walked away.

"Number 12 please go back to your bench," called an assistant.

I was leaning against one of the fridges with my back to the cooking area. "I don't feel good," I told her as she stood in front of me. "I need something to drink."

She looked at my face and saw me bent over. "All right, I'll get you some juice." A moment later I was sitting on the ground when she handed me a small bottle of orange juice. "Dionne is tasting your food now. Pull yourself together and get back to your bench."

I watched her retreating back and wondered why she was being so rude when I was feeling so sick. After finishing off the juice, I slowly climbed to my feet and walked back to the bench. The food, especially the bugs, had been eaten, and I noticed some of the other contestants looking green around the gills.

"You have all excelled at this," Dionne said. "Now, impress us with lunch."

I glanced around the room at the cameras and lights, the people running around still licking their lips. "Ugh." I read the recipes and decided to go with something that sounded easy. Fish head stew. Problem was, when I got to the fridge the fish was still whole, dead fortunately, but whole. I carried the tray back to the bench and went for the other ingredients.

I'd never chopped a full fish up before, and this time I had to scale, de-bone, and chop up the body too. Luckily one of the assistants came to help me. It looked as though we were able to get help, as I noticed several others being helped too.

I filled up the stew pot with water, added salt, and dumped in the head, sliced up the fillets the assistant had done for me, and made a marinade to soak them in. While the marinade was part of the recipe, I decided to add an extra ingredient of my own to it. I chopped up the weird looking vegetables and added them to the bubbling water, sprinkled in some herbs and spices I'd never heard of, and freaked out when the head bobbed to the surface. I guiltily looked around and noticed sick expressions on everyone else's faces. *Where did they get this stuff from?* I wondered. *And who eats it?*

I was certainly *not* going to taste it to see if it was ready, but fortunately Dionne saved me from that. Tasting the stew, she greedily licked her lips. "Time to add the fish." She moved on, then turned back. "But turn it off after putting it in, wait two minutes then serve."

"Okay." I grabbed the plate of fish strips and slid them into the pot. At the two minute mark I scooped some into a bowl and served it up ready for tasting.

Blaaaaaaaaaaaaarrrrrrrrrrrrrr.

The siren sounded and Dionne clapped her hands. "Assistants, move in."

Fifty or so people in chefs' uniforms converged on twelve benches devouring food, licking plates, and drinking from bowls. Blech!

I was not only dumbfounded, but horrified and disgusted by what I saw. The twelve of us contestants all moved to the side and huddled together.

"What are they doing? They look like animals," contestant number 3 said.

"What is going on?" number 7 added.

"I feel sick." Number 9 hurled into a nearby bin.

"Darcy." Jen grabbed my arm. "It's a feeding frenzy of wild animals. What's going on?"

"Don't know, Jen, but I'm scared." My insides were a quivering mass of jelly, and I wanted to run out the door and not look back. They hadn't been like that the last three days, but then maybe they were building up to it. This was definitely *not* what I signed up for.

"They look like animals, Darcy," Jen whispered.

Dionne and her assistants stopped. Heads slowly rose, forked tongues slowly licked, and heads slowly turned toward the twelve of us huddled off to the side.

"*Wonderful,* children, just...*wonderful.*" Dionne placed her bowl on the bench and turned to us. She straightened her uniform and hair before dabbing at her mouth with a napkin. "Now, show us what you can do with dessert."

I really could not face making another meal out of weird exotic bugs and fish. Ugh, I felt sick. Jen and I reluctantly let go of each other and we all slowly trooped back to our benches. I read the dessert recipes and *did* want to be sick, but found one that didn't seem to require dead animals. I collected my ingredients along with everyone else who seemed to have the same idea…to stay away from dead animals.

It seemed like a normal berry pie and I needed a crunchy biscuit base for it. The biscuits were weird and as I broke them up, they already sounded crunchy and smelled a little. After filling a plastic bag with the crumbs, I tied it and ran a rolling pin over it before pouring the crumbs into a bowl. I added butter and a few pinches of secret ingredient, and rubbed it all together. After coating the inside of the two martini glasses with the weird biscuit base, I put them in the fridge to harden.

The berry mixture went into a saucepan on high and I added a touch of sugar, some vanilla bean, the juices of one lemon, one lime, and an orange, and mixed it until the berries melted, and moved…and grew legs and heads then dissolved…

"Ewww." The chorus was heard around the room as the others saw what I just had.

"Don't worry, children," Dionne soothed. "Very special bug berries from a very special country. They die when they dissolve. Keep cooking." She stood to one side watching us.

"Ugh." I let my mixture cool down, then not only

got my glasses from the fridge, but a juice as well. I downed it in one go, feeling sick and hot and thirsty. I poured the mixture into the glasses and laid on a dollop of a cream/ice cream mix I'd made up, then sprinkled the zest of lemon, lime and orange over it. After washing my hands in the sink with sanitiser, I stood back and wiped them, waiting for it to be over.

Blaaaaaaaaaaaarrrrrrrrrrrr.

"Assistants," Dionne called. "Let's eat."

Once again we contestants huddled off to the side of the room, watching the feeding frenzy that was now dessert time.

"I don't want to win, Darcy," Jen whispered.

I returned her scared look. "Neither do I." We heard some murmurings behind us and saw they all felt the same.

Waiting until they were finished and had placed bowls and glasses down and licked lips and fingers, Dionne and her crew turned to us. "There are only two clear winners of this heat who will go through to cook for the title of the *Trifest Children's Master Cook Masterclass Cooking Competition*...and they are...numbers 1 and 12." We all looked down at our numbers and heard the chorus of thank gods behind us.

"The rest of you may go."

We felt the wind gush around us as the other ten contestants raced for the door.

"Numbers 1 and 12." Dionne glided over to us, hands clasped in front of her, eyes glassed over. "We have very special recipes for you tomorrow.

We wish you luck. Now go home and rest."

Jen and I clung to each other for grim death under the glares and gazes of everyone in the room. "Okay," we managed before following our fellow competitors out the door.

*****

We stood in front of the Master Cook hangar the next morning, clinging to each other and not moving from the spot where we'd been dropped off.

"I feel sick, Jen." I hadn't slept all night and was sick in the bathroom before leaving.

"Same here." She dug her nails into my arm. "I don't want to be here, Darce, I'm scared. I thought you were joking about their tongues and stuff, but after yesterday…now I'm wondering if they're even human."

We stared up at the huge Master Cook logo flag at the top of the building. A cool breeze wafted through the air and ruffled it slightly along with our aprons.

"Darcy, Jennifer." An assistant came forward. "Time for the competition."

We stood rooted to the ground and didn't follow her, which she noticed and came back to us. "Inside… now," she hissed, a bizarre combination expression of anger, frustration and…evil on her off white, almost iridescent green face.

"Ah," we cried out and meekly followed.

Run Darcy, run, floated through my brain, and I

desperately wanted to, but my feet kept moving me forward. Forward until we stood in front of two benches.

The assistants and crew crowded us as we stood shaking and rooted to the spot.

"Darcy, Jennifer." Dionne drifted toward us all perfect in her uniform. "We have chosen you as the two winners to battle it out for the top prize. We have taken great interest in your recipes, especially the added touches and ingredients you've used to make it your own. And an even greater interest in the way you made yesterday's recipes unique from everyone else. But today…is different." She stood in front of us looking down with extra-large glassy, almost unnatural looking eyes.

We shivered under her gaze and I nearly vomited.

"Today you get to use even more delicacies from our home planet, uh, country," she quickly corrected herself.

Jen and I glanced curiously at each other.

"We will watch over you closely, helping you where needed, hoping your secret ingredients will get you over the line." She clapped her hands twice. "Now, the first recipe is Bung Chew Bah, a delicious meal of eggs and Bung Bah bugs." She turned and waved a hand in the direction of the benches. "The ingredients are already waiting, so please read your recipes and get started."

Taking deep breaths, Jen and I reluctantly headed for our benches. In front of me was a huge pot of water simmering away, a huge bowl of large black bug creatures, and a bowl of eggs. And I mean *large* eggs. Like emu or ostrich or something. *As in the size of my head eggs!* There was a small bowl of dried ingredients. I picked up the recipe and read it. "Take the bugs and boil for five minutes, add the crushed spices, and five minutes later crack three eggs into the pot and simmer until done."

I looked at the basket of bugs.

"They are already dead," Dionne told us, hovering in front of our worktops.

Jen and I looked at each other, then at the crowd around us, the crowd that surrounded us, almost suffocated us. I picked up the basket and put the bug like creatures into the water.

"Eeeeeek. Eeeeeeek."

I jumped back. "Argh."

"Sorry." Dionne nonchalantly waved a hand. "Must have just stunned them before, they'll be dead in five minutes."

Jen and I exchanged a sick to our stomach glance as everyone licked their lips with their forked tongues. *All of them* had forked tongues. What had we gotten ourselves into?

We added the spices. "Phwoar, that stinks." I waved my hand in front of my face to fend off the nasty stench invading my nostrils.

"That's crushed Chew Choi and Bung Boo."

"What?" I asked through watering eyes while holding my nose.

"Insects from our planet," Dionne replied bluntly.

I looked up. "Planet?"

Dionne met my stare. "Time for the eggs. Crack them straight into the pot."

I looked at Jen, which I was doing a lot of. Something was so wrong, but I didn't know what to do. Our parents weren't there to help us, and we had no way of getting away and calling anyone. And even if we did, I doubted we could get far in this building with all these people who were basically standing guard over us.

We picked up an egg each. I cracked mine and pulled the shell apart. A small mewling creature with weird screwed up, buckled arms and legs cried out. "Bahhh!" I jumped back as it fell into the pot. "*What was that?*" I screamed.

The assistants crowded around as did Jen.

"What *was* that? *Was that an animal?*" I cried. "*A live animal?*" I backed away in terror, but they closed in around me, moving me back to the bench.

Dionne sighed. "Of course it was, now crack the others into the pot so they can cook."

I vehemently shook my head. "No. No. What *are* you weirdos? Wanting to cook live baby animals. This is horrible. I *will not do this.*" The assistants crowded in closer.

"You have to do it, Darcy," Dionne hissed. "We *need* you to do this." Her forked tongue slid out and waved around. She grabbed the second egg and cracked it into the pot, then the third. Her eyes grew bigger and her fingers extended. Her skin dissolved to reveal green scale-like things underneath until she had shed her exterior human skin to reveal who, or what, she truly was beneath.

Jennifer screamed along with me, and we ran to each other, hanging on for fear of death. An early death I did not need...or want. *What are you? What is this?* I cried.

"I want to go home, Darcy," Jen added beside me.

"You *are* home girls," Dionne hissed, and waved her hands at her assistants. They followed Dionne and shed their human skin to reveal green reptilian skin and forked tongues. They edged towards us, pushing us against my bench.

"We needed new chefs to cook for us back on our home planet because our old ones...died..." She waved a hand. "They ran out of ways to recreate our unique recipes and so they needed to...go... And because I'm in the public eye and known worldwide, I get to find new cooks via a competition." Her tongue weaved towards us.

"Argh." We leapt back but felt the tongues behind us. "Argh." We jumped forward.

"We chose you two because you are young and will become one of us easily when you get to our planet." The siren sounded. "In the meantime. Let's eat."

THE DEAD PEOPLE

My eyes fluttered open against the darkness of the room. It smelt. A dark, mouldy smell, emanating from every pore of the walls and floor. I waited until my eyes adjusted to the darkness before moving my head.

Where am I? What is this place?

My fingers inched along the space beside me, finding what I thought were blankets. A pillow was under my head, and I found chain above me. Fingers gently touched the links and followed them until they found the bolt attached to the wall.

I turned slowly and quietly, hoping to stay silent as I had no idea if I was alone or someone, or something, else, was in the room with me.

Once on my side, I saw a sliver of light glowing under what could be a door. Would it be locked?

What do I do?

My body ached and creaked with every movement I made. I had to go slow; I had to be quiet. "Ah," I gasped, going against the plan to make no noise. The pain seared up my leg and raced through my spine to my skull.

What in…ugh…where did that come from?

I rested a moment, waiting for the ring of pain to settle and then moved again. One leg off the side of the bed. Two legs off the bed and heading for the floor. Arms slowly pushing their body up off the bed and into a sitting position.

Ugh, dizzy…the room…spinning…left, right, it won't stop.

I bent forward and put my head in my hands. The dizziness calmed, slowed down from a tornado to a mild storm, and finally to a light wind. Taking a deep breath, I inched toward the wall at the end of the bed, unsure if there even was a wall.

I found it, and slowly walked along, waving my other hand out in front of me to find anything before I bumped into it. I hit another wall, and followed it to my left until I felt metal and hinges and found the door knob.

"Ouch!"

I whipped my hand toward my mouth and furiously blew on it. It was boiling hot. The handle had been heated, presumably so I couldn't get out. Waving my hand, I wondered what I could use to cover the handle. Maybe a pillow case or blanket or something. Inching my way back to the bed, I felt for the pillow and found a cover I could pull off. I wrapped the case around my hand, returned to the door, grasped the knob and turned.

And turned…

And turned…

No matter which way I turned the handle the

door remained closed.

Bugger! It's locked.

Click clack click clack.

The sound came toward the door and stopped right out front. No time for being careful; I ran straight across the room and threw myself onto the bed with a pounding heart and pretended to be asleep.

Clang…clang…click…

The door opened with an almighty creak and light spilled into the small room. I opened one eye and glanced around. I may have been facing the wall, but I could see the light on the wall above me with an ominous shadow dancing in its midst.

Click clack click clack…they came closer…

Bang, thud, rattle.

The sound was right behind me.

"Baaaahhh!" An electric current ran through me and I sprang up, rolling over on the bed. "What was that?" I yelped, putting my hand over the spot on my arm.

"I gave you a shock," came the strange metallic and grating voice. "When people are doing something wrong, we touch them and send a thousand volts through their bodies."

I gazed upon the being before me. The thing that had spoken was distorted, big-eyed, and deformed. Maybe my height, with long thin arms and fingers, but short fat legs and feet, it looked like a pear with a lollipop for a head.

"What…in the…blazes…" I breathed. I was scared

out of my wits and freaking out in fear at the…the…the *thing* standing before me, surrounded by a halo of light from the hallway.

"I am Zapper," it said without moving its mouth. "I am a Zoid."

"A what?"

"A Zoid."

"What's…a…Zoid?"

"An alien, as you may know us."

"Oh." Well, I had kinda figured that out, but squashed against the cold stone wall of a teeny tiny room while this *thing* was in front of me speaking without opening its mouth was *really* freaking me out. "Where am I?"

"You are still on the planet Earth." It blinked and added a slight tilt of its head. "You are underground. We brought you here while you were asleep."

I remembered back. Hadn't I been in my house in my bed? "Where are my parents?"

"They are here too, working in one of the caves."

"How did we get here?" Had it been in the usual alien abduction way?

"We hovered over your house and beamed you up."

Yep, the usual alien abduction way!

"I have brought you some food. You must be hungry, and we need to keep your strength up."

"Why are we here? Why did you abduct us?" I glanced at the tray of goop. A glass of clear liquid stood next to the plate.

It blinked. "Our people are slowly dying and we

need human energy. We need parts of the human body. That is why I brought you food. So we can store up your energy."

I gulped. "You need parts of the human body? What for?" Did I really want to know the answer to my own question?

"To replace our own."

"Ugh, what?" I stared dumbfounded. "How do you mean, *replace* our own?" It could not have been what I was thinking of.

Blink... "When our hearts, lungs or brain fails we need another to transplant. But we don't have any so we need more and human body parts are almost like ours. So we'll be taking what we want."

"Wait," I called as it turned. "What does *that* mean? I'm not the only one you abducted. Is this an invasion...of the whole country...?"

"The whole planet, actually." It click-clacked out the door.

"Wait." I panicked. "There's no air in here, how am I able to breathe?"

"You will be all right. Oxygen is being fed through pipes."

"What about light? I can't see to eat or anything." I was over-panicking now, not wanting him to go, but not wanting him to stay.

He flicked his hand against the wall to the side of the door and the overhead bulb came on.

"Oh." I hadn't found that before.

He closed the door and click-clacked away.

Gazing around the room, I saw it was bare except

for the bed hanging off the wall and a small table to the side. I looked at the food and moved closer. My stomach growled and I leaned in for a sniff.

Mmmm mashed potato and gravy…

I picked up the spoon and poked at the other things on the plate. Green mush, thick brown goop…mmm…gravy…it can't be my favourite foods. I picked up the plate and held it under the yellow light from the bulb. *Looks like mash and gravy and mushy peas or something.* I tasted a bit of each. *Tastes like mash and gravy and mushy peas.*

I was famished and couldn't help myself any longer. I shovelled that food into my mouth so fast I was done in thirty seconds. I dropped the plate on the tray and picked up the glass, studying it under the light as well.

Looks like water…smells like water…wait, what does water smell like? *Tastes like water…*I took a chance and gulped it down.

Once I was finished I searched the room. What for I wasn't sure, but I figured I'd better. I stared at the door pondering my next move. *Should I try opening it again? Will it still be hot? What will happen if it opens? Where am I? How will I get out? Where are my parents?*

Knowing I had to take another chance, I grabbed the pillow case and wound it around my hand. Moulding my hand around the knob, I turned and heard the click of release. I flicked off the light and slowly opened the door, keeping my ears open for any sound and my eyes open for any Zoids.

I was in a tunnel, carved out of dirt and stone. Opening the door wider, I stuck my head out. There was a door opposite me and many more to the left and right. Small light globes hung above each door illuminating their cold metal darkness.

Click clack click clack.

I ducked back into the room and held the door open just a crack. Two more Zoids walked past pulling a cart behind them. It was a cart full of humans, dead looking, yet somehow still breathing humans.

I waited for them to pass before silently following them to a huge wooden door. I ducked into a crevice and watched them knock three times from my hiding place.

"Password?" a voice called through the intercom.

"Humans," one Zoid answered.

The door unlocked and opened and, as they carted their human pile through, I saw a big spaceship beyond.

Blimey!

I quickly pondered what to do and knew I had to find my parents and rescue as many people as I could. Making as little noise as possible, I ran from door to door down the long tunnel, grabbing each knob with my pillow case covered hand, and freeing children, teens and adults. They were stunned, disorientated, and unsure of what to do.

But then, so was I.

"Listen," I whispered to the crowd now gathered in the tunnel. "There's a door down the other end that leads to a huge room with a spaceship. I'm not sure what we can do with that, but I want to find my parents. One of those things told me they were working in a cave. I need to find them."

"What about *my* parents?" Tim piped up. He was my next door neighbour and we hung out and rode our bikes together sometimes. "Mine aren't here either." He glanced at the crowd. From the look of it none of us was related to anyone else. That meant kids had no parents, and parents had no kids. All of us were alone.

"I say we keep together and find a way out," Mrs Fenech, the high school physics teacher, said as she brushed her clothes down. "Safety in numbers, and we adults need to look after the kids."

Mr Tomlinson disagreed. "I think we should split up."

"There's no point," Mrs Fenech argued. "If we split up one group gets out and one doesn't. Or none of us gets out."

"Stop," I whispered furiously, making them shut up and look at me. "Look, the Zoids came from that way." I pointed down the tunnel behind me. "I say we follow them and free anyone else that may be trapped. I'm going." I stared at the others in defiance. "Who's with me?" I got a few grumbles in return but turned my back and headed off down the tunnel anyway.

Moving quickly and quietly, we stuck to the walls and looked down any tunnels we came across. We found more doors and freed more people, none of whom were my parents. We found our way into a cave and stood staring at the scene before us.

At least one hundred bodies were there, all mechanically moving, but dead in every other way. Their eyes were empty black holes; their bodies, limp and rubber-like. Like Gumby. It was as if they had no skeletons holding them up yet somehow, were able to move.

We crowded behind some crates and watched as I looked for my parents. None of these people looked like them, and I feared I would never find them.

"Mum, Dad," Tim yelled and ran out from behind a crate to the female and male bodies his parents now were.

"Tim," I hissed. "Get back here." I raced after him, ducking behind crates and humans until I came face to face with the things, the empty shells that were no longer his parents.

"Mum? Dad?" Tears fell silently down Tim's cheeks as he stood before them, waiting for recognition.

"They're gone," I whispered, grabbing his arm. "Let's go, they're not your parents anymore. They've been taken over by the Zoids. Come on." I dragged him away crying and kicking.

"Mummy, Daddy," he screamed over and over.

"Shut up, Tim, you'll bring the Zoids." I hauled him back behind the crates and told the others. "We gotta get out of here before they catch us."

With one last look at the mechanical non-humans, we ran out of the room.

Dark, dank tunnel after dark, dank tunnel. More

rooms, more people, dead and alive. I knew most of the survivors from my neighbourhood and area, but still didn't find my parents.

Using the buddy system, we crept down another tunnel until we came to a fork. With three tunnels to pick from, we were more lost than ever before.

I glanced around in despair. "Anyone have any ideas?" I whispered.

"I say we keep going up. The tunnel has ascended, and if we go up, we should find a way out," a balding middle-aged man said.

We looked down the tunnel on our left. Was that a breeze?

"I smell fresh air," Mrs Fenech said under her breath. "It might be a way out."

"Then go," I replied. "Get out, all of you. I'm going to look for my parents, but you lot go and hide when you get outside, or run away, or whatever you can." I turned for the tunnel on our right, but Mr Tomlinson stepped in.

"You can't go on your own. We should all get out now, so come on."

I watched everyone huddled together. "No, I have to find my parents."

"The kid's right, we need to find as many survivors as possible and put those rat finks out of business. Who knows how many are down here." The man who stepped forward was big, bulky, and square-jawed.

"And who are *you* to tell us that? I've never seen you before." Mr Tomlinson didn't like being told what to do, especially by someone he didn't know.

Crash…thud…the sounds came from the distant right and several survivors cried out.

"The name's Studmore. Henry Studmore. Fifth Para Military Brigade, Vietnam, Iraq. Let's split up and put these rat finks out of commission."

I'd had enough of the time wasting. "Look, the women can take the children outside and run or hide. Some of the men go with them to protect them; the rest can come with me or leave. There's no more time to waste." I stormed off down the right tunnel and heard footsteps behind me. Mr Studmore was following, with older teenagers and other men. In the distance I saw the rest of the group becoming smaller and smaller as they left through the tunnel behind us.

We came upon cave after cave of dead people; black soulless holes where eyes should be, pallid skin, boneless bodies. As we went on down, down, down, deeper into the dark depths of the underground world, I was grabbed and hauled against the wall.

"Whoa—" A hand covered my mouth.

We flattened against dirt and stone at the click-clacking in the distance, watching as two Zoids dragged their cart of human bodies across the tunnel fifteen feet ahead of us.

"We should follow them," was murmured in my ear, and after being let go, I turned my head to see it was Mr Studmore who'd grabbed me.

I nodded. "We need to get to the spaceship and do something. I need to find my parents." With a nod from him, and a hand gesture from me to those behind us, we set off down the tunnel the aliens had taken.

Walking for several minutes, we noticed the tunnel growing wider and wider before opening up into a ginormous cavern.

I didn't even realise I had barged right into the cave until I was thrown behind some crates. With a nod of thanks for the rescue, I ducked down with the others and crept along till we were away from the entrance.

"We shouldn't be seen here," Studmore murmured.

Studying our surroundings we saw the usual shaped UFO, Zoids moving crates and carts and dead people all around. Just a few didn't look so dead.

Mum, Dad! I sprang up, but was pulled back down.

"I see them too." Studmore put his fingers to his lips. "But we need to be quick and quiet."

I silently agreed and kept my mouth closed. Peering over the boxes, we slowly moved around the room. Jars and containers were piled on the boxes and filled with human samples. Spines, hearts, livers and kidneys; basically every inside part of a human being. We saw tables with bodies without skin, some without skeletons, being kept alive by the tubing stuck in every limb. The odour wafting toward us was putrid and really revolting.

I read the words on each crate, a language not of this Earth, not of our kind, a language only Zoids spoke as they loaded crate after crate into their ship.

We made it most of the way around and I could see the humans more clearly. The non-dead ones that is; the ones still very much alive and very much human. My parents were filling boxes and containers into the crates and nailing them shut. I made a move, but Studmore pulled me back.

He put his mouth to my ear. "Say nothing to them, use hand signals instead. Make no sudden moves."

I looked at him and nodded. After carefully crawling the last few metres, I peeked my head from behind a crate and tried to get my parents' attention. It took a few minutes of waiting, but Dad finally saw me. His eyes widened and he seemed to panic, but I shook my head and put my finger to my lips, warning him to be quiet.

"Get back to work," a grating voice told him, and I withdrew to wait for another opportunity.

A few minutes later I had it. Dad used his eyes to signal to an open box about ten metres in front of me. I nodded and pointed it out to Studmore. We got into position to study the box and the light dawned on him. He made the hand gestures of lighting a big stick and then kaboom.

Dynamite? I mouthed and he gave me the thumbs up. We withdrew to make plans.

After waiting for the right moment, Studmore hunched down, sped to the open box and hid behind it, giving me another thumbs up after checking its contents. The rest of us huddled together and I signalled to my parents who kept an eye out when they could.

Putting as much dynamite as possible in his shirt he set upon his mission and moved on. I took my chance to run behind the dynamite box as well, tucking my shirt into my pants and then filling it with as many sticks as I could. I raced back to the others.

Studmore had left us with a pack of matches as he liked a good puff on a cigar occasionally and had a few packs in his pants pocket. I shared the dynamite and matches out, and signalled to my parents. Then I waited.

Kaboom!

The first stick went off and the Zoids went running. I waved my parents over. They grabbed the others and made a run for us. After hugging quickly, we ignited more dynamite and left sticks every ten paces along the crates. We made our way back to the cave entrance and met up with Studmore who came from the opposite direction.

Kaboom kaboom kaboom kaboom kaboom…

Explosion after explosion ripped apart the spaceship, as crates of body parts went flying into the air and so did Zoids.

The ship collapsed as the legs blew off and we made a run for it.

"Attention, attention, prisoners have escaped. Prisoners have escaped."

Electrical blasts hit the wall behind us and Studmore lit and threw more dynamite; not only at the Zoids chasing us, but down every tunnel we passed.

Kaboom kaboom kaboom…

We hit the deck after one explosion and had dirt, debris and green goop rain down on us.

"Adam, Martha, let's go." Dad moved us up and forward as we all hustled along the tunnel.

More dynamite, more explosions, more dead Zoids.

Running for our lives, we made our way out of the tunnel and into the bright daylight of our alien-ruined world.

Studmore threw the last sticks of burning dynamite into the tunnel and we ran, dashing for the group of people waving to us from the forest ahead of us. We kept running until we got to them, and found it was the rest of our group.

I threw myself down onto the ground, and my Mum and Dad threw themselves on top of me, hugging and kissing me. We huddled as a family, with Dad holding both me and Mum, and when I glanced around I found small groups doing the same. We stayed that way as a small group, although we were probably a hundred or so people with all the survivors we'd found.

I looked back at the cave as a massive rumbling spread across the land. We hung on, worried it was an earthquake, but an explosion ripped through from below and the tunnels we had just come from imploded. It looked as if the spaceship had exploded on itself, but I wasn't going to go and look at the ginormous pit the size of the Grand Canyon that now took up the wasteland.

I felt my stomach lurch, and made it over to a

tree before barfing my guts up, bringing up mess after mess.

Gee, I thought as I rested a moment, *it must have been the food!*

RAT FINKS

"Mum, we're gonna go ride our bikes," Mike called out as we ran down the stairs and out the front door.

"Whoa, hold up a minute."

We stopped and turned as the screen door slammed against the wall of the house.

"You're not going anywhere. Haven't you heard the reports that a couple of boys have gone missing in town?" She stood on the porch wiping her hands on a towel.

Mike and I looked at each other and rolled our eyes. "Mum that was on the other side of town, far, far away. It's not here. We're going to the local park a few streets over. We'll be fine," I said.

"Besides," Mike added. "*You're* the one who moved us here and wants us to make friends and stuff, so we need to go ride our bikes." We watched her standing there, knowing we were right. Our mum had moved us across the country so she could start her new job. She'd told us to get out and about to meet kids our own age, but now wanted us to stay in just because some kids had gone missing.

She relented. "You got your phones?" We nodded. "Call me if anything happens or goes wrong. Be home by five." Her voice faded as we rode away.

We cruised down our street, made a left turn onto the main road, and continued until we came to the big park and oval attached to our new school. It had skateboard and bike ramps, a small basketball court and a seating area. We rode up and sat watching the kids doing 360 spins and backflips on their bikes.

"Hey." A kid our age rode over. "Haven't seen you here before."

We gave him the once over. "New, moved in last week, start school in the new term," Mike replied, turning back to look at the tricks being performed.

I continued watching the kid. "What's *your* name?"

"Chris," he replied with a nod at us. "And you two?"

"I'm David; he's Mike." I flicked a finger in my brother's direction.

"Cool." Blond Chris shrugged. "Wanna come join?"

Mike glanced at me and gave a slight nod of approval. "Sure."

For the next couple of hours we met the kids and talked about local stuff before talk turned to the missing boys.

"Apparently they were our age." Chris dumped his bike on the grass and sat a couple of metres away. The other kids followed his lead as if he was the boss of the group, so Mike and I did too.

"My Mum said she knows one of the mothers from some group she's in," a skinny red-haired boy said. I think his name was Red; at least that's what some of the others had called him. "The cops think her son ran away, but she says he went to his friend's place and never came back."

"I heard some boys from the next town over disappeared as well. The news thinks there's some cult or serial killer on the loose going after kids our age." The kid talking was a good looking brunet, a little older than me, maybe Mike's age, and all the girls hovering around seemed to be at the oval only for him. "So, what do you two think?" He nodded in our direction. "You're the newbies."

Mike and I looked at each other before eyeing off everyone else. "Well," Mike started before leaning back on his hands. "We just moved here, so don't know much about it. Anyone know whether they ran away, or were taken by someone?"

I sat cross-legged next to him and scratched my leg. It was getting itchy from the grass, and the sun was beating down and making me sweat.

Everyone in the group looked at everyone else. Apparently no one had the answer.

"Does *no one* know what actually happened to them, or the other kids?" Mike glanced around. "Has *no one* looked it up yet?"

Shrugs went around the group. "Why do we need to know?" the good-looking kid asked. "It's got nothing to do with us."

I hadn't heard anyone say his name, so I had no idea what it was.

Mike sat up. "Because we're kids, and if kids are

being targeted, then we need to be on the lookout for strangers in town. Adults who might be hanging around kids' parks, etc, unless you want to be kidnapped..."

The kids shared another glance and then stared at Mike and me. "No," they murmured one by one.

"Well," Mike said. "Let's start a neighbourhood watch then."

*****

Meeting back at the oval the next day, this time we were armed with food, water, hats, sunscreen and long pants. No way was I going to get grass itch again!

Sitting in a circle, we shared what information we had learned.

"I googled last night and found ten more kids who are missing," Chris said. "All our ages, and all from across the country."

"We had visitors last night, and one was the sister of a missing kid's mum. Apparently he went to a friend's house and never went home. The friend and his family were questioned, but the cops think it happened on his way home," the good-looking brunet kid, who we now knew as Gary, answered.

"All the times of the disappearances seem to be around or just after sunset when the kids are supposed to be going home," Red added. "Maybe that's when the kidnapper strikes?"

Several others agreed.

"So, we need to be home by five then." Mike scratched his arm. "If we wanna stay safe, then we'd better be home by dark."

"But what about sports practice once school starts?" a little kid piped up. "We all do sport for school."

"School doesn't start for another few weeks, so we'll be safe till then," I added to the conversation before shrugging. "After that, we'll have to come up with another plan."

"Maybe our parents will be able to drive us?" Manny mumbled around a sandwich.

"Or we could bike pool, you know, instead of carpool, we all ride together, or in small groups if we live in the same area," Gary chimed in. "I live south, so any kids that live in that area can ride with me." He seemed to relish the role he'd given himself as sudden leader of the group. He was one of the older and bigger members of the fifty or so kids sitting around on the grass.

"I'm north, so anyone else from north?" Red asked. About ten put their hands up. "Then we can ride together too."

Kids from the east and west sorted themselves out, but the easties were worried. "Two kids have already gone missing in our area, so maybe we should just stay home until school starts," one kid said.

"And be sookie boys?" Gary said. "Sookie sookie la lahs. Just coz two kids went missing doesn't mean you will. Or any of us." He stood up and flexed his muscles. "If anyone comes near me and tries something, I'll give 'em the old one-two." He danced around, punching at imaginary foes. "Yes, siree, no one's gonna mess with Gary Tackle."

After another hour of Gary's windbagness, we rode home, dumped our bikes on the lawn, and went in search of food and drink. We found Mum in the kitchen wiping down the benches after baking.

"How was the park?" She removed her apron and gave it a shake out over the sink.

"Good." I got two cans of soda from the fridge and threw one at Mike who was sitting at the kitchen bench. "Hot," I added, after sculling back a few mouthfuls.

"Making friends then?"

"Yeah." Mike put his can down. "But now they've set up a neighbourhood watch kinda thing, where kids from the same area all bike pool to the park and back to keep an eye on each other."

Mum finished folding her apron. "That sounds like an interesting idea, especially with what happened to those two boys." Brushing off her hands, she added, "Dinner's in the oven, so you'll have to wait an hour or so. Are you joining their neighbourhood watch group?"

Mike grabbed an apple from the fruit bowl. "Figured we may as well since we're new to the area and should keep an eye on how things work."

She nodded. "Yes, definitely keep an eye out, and let me know if you see anyone acting inappropriately and I'll check them out."

Mum was a Sergeant in the last town we were in

and knew people in our new place, but this time she'd be working in the local politician's office and was starting in a week.

*****

A couple of days later, we were back at the park and found some of the boys fighting.

"What's going on?" We pulled to a stop alongside Chris as Gary tackled Red.

"A kid went missing from north last night, and Gary's blaming Red for not doing anything to stop it, or prevent it."

I glanced from Chris to Mike who pulled a funny looking can with a horn on it from his bag.

Walking over to the two boys, he held it out in front of them and pressed the button. The earsplitting horn rang loud and long, stopping the two boys in their tracks and making the rest of us block our ears. Mike released the button. "What *are* you two doing? Another kid is missing and *you're* fighting."

Gary's attitude boiled over. "Who *are you* to stop a fight?" He placed both hands on Mike's chest and shoved him backwards. "Blowing a horn in our faces." He sneered in Mike's face. "Yeah, a kid is missing, and it's Red's fault because he was the leader of the northies. They were supposed to be looking out for each other." Another shove. "But clearly, Red didn't care."

Mike stepped back and half turned to throw the horn at me before facing off against Gary. "Red is not to blame any more than the rest of us, and fighting him *won't* and *doesn't* help. Neither does shoving me."

Gary shoved him anyway.

Mike sighed. "That's three strikes, Gary."

Gary sneered; it was clearly a permanent thing, besides his ego. "Three strikes for what?" He stuck his bottom lip out. "Pushing you? What, are you going to cwy wike a widdle baby?" He put his hands up ready to shove again, but Mike did the unexpected. Well, unexpected for Gary that is. I already knew it was coming.

Mike turned, grabbed Gary's left arm, and threw him over his shoulder and flat onto the ground. He turned again and yanked Gary's arm up behind his back. "*That's* what happens when your three strikes are up, Gary. I flatten you."

Gary yelled in pain and everyone just stood around in shock. Chris looked at me with eyes the size of saucers. I shrugged. "Our Mum's an ex-cop; she taught us self-defence."

Mike yanked Gary's arm again, getting an animalistic growl in return. "Yes, she did," he said, leaning down. "She also taught us to defend other people against bullies." He threw Gary's hand down. "And *you* were being a bully." He stepped away and turned to Red. "Is it true? A kid from the north went missing last night?" Red nodded. "Well, it's not your fault. We're kids; we can only do so much."

"Arrrgghhhh…"

Mike easily outmanoeuvred the growling Gary

who'd sprung up from the ground and charged at him. A swift side step and a simple hand movement, and Gary face-planted the green grass of the oval.

*****

We told Mum about Gary's bad behaviour when we got home. "He was just being a bully." I munched on a meat and cheese sandwich. "But Mike showed him what for."

"Mike," she scolded as she walked in from the laundry with a mop and bucket. "I taught you self-defence to defend yourself and your brother—"

"And people who needed defending," I added.

She dropped everything on the floor and relented. "Was he beating up this kid, Red?"

"Yep," we replied in unison.

"Then it sounds like this Gary needed to be taught a lesson." She dunked the mop into the bucket that was full of soapy water. "Why don't you invite this Gary over tomorrow afternoon?" She slapped the mop back and forth across the kitchen floor. "And I'll have some of my special cookies waiting."

*****

We rolled up to the park and caught up on all the details with Chris. Turns out, the missing kid had gone to a friend's place and not returned. A search was made after his parents reported him missing, but so far nothing had been found.

"Looks like they're being nabbed on their way home," I told Chris while we watched Mike back flip on his bike. My brother loved his BMX and could trick it with the best of them. "Maybe the perp finds a kid and then follows him everywhere, gets to know his schedule, and then pounces when they're alone."

"Perp?" Chris gave me a funny look. "You've been watching *way* too many crime shows, dude."

I gave a small laugh. "Yeah, I guess I have." We heard shouting and turned to see Gary furiously riding across the grass toward us. He pulled to a stop, threw his bike down, and stormed onto the middle of the bike ramp where Mike skidded to a halt in front of him.

"What *are* you doing?" Mike asked, taking off his helmet.

"I told my parents what you did to me and they're going to sue you for it. You had no right to throw me over your shoulder and flatten me out." He slammed his hands onto his hips and made himself as large as he could. We knew from Mum this was an intimidation tactic, but it didn't bother Mike who casually looked in my direction.

"I did that because you were beating up Red and he didn't deserve it. I was defending him against *you*. *You're* a bully Gary, that's why I did it."

Gary sneered, which seemed to be a thing he did a lot. "Yeah, right. Like anyone here is going to say I was doing anything." He glanced around. "I didn't do anything, did I boys?"

I looked at their faces as they lowered theirs. Fear, shock, disbelief. And one angry one. Red. I could tell he wanted to stand up for himself, but just didn't have the wherewithal.

Gary faced off against Mike. "See, *I* didn't do anything, but *you* did." He poked a finger in Mike's chest. "So my parents are suing you and your parents."

Mike threw another glance my way. I knew what was coming. "Why don't you come over this afternoon? We can talk about it over Mum's special chocolate chip cookies. She says we should invite our new friends over…"

"Friends?" The sneer on Gary's face was perpetually etched. But it softened. "Chocolate chip cookies…"

"*Special*…chocolate chip cookies," Mike repeated.

Gary gulped and licked his lips. "Okay…deal… now I'm gonna beat you at BMX tricks." He ran over and got his bike and Mike gave me a small nod.

I wandered away and sent a quick text to Mum that Gary would be coming for cookies.

*****

After a few hours of Gary and Mike going toe to toe at BMX biking, we left the others and rode home. We lived less than a kilometre away, which was handy since we were straight down the road from the school. When the time came for us to go back, it would take less than ten minutes to get there.

We led Gary around the back of the house and left our bikes leaning against the porch steps. Bursting into the kitchen, we saw icy cold cola and a plate of fresh out of the oven cookies steaming on the counter.

Before Mike and I could even get any Gary pulled the plate in front of him and shoved several into his mouth. "Oh…muh…gah…so…good…" His eyes closed against the heaven that was Mum's special choc chip cookies, especially when they're fresh out of the oven and melting in your mouth.

Mike and I sat at the kitchen bench drinking our sodas, and watching Gary all but inhale the whole plate of biscuits. He finished them off by sculling back his soda and burping loudly…just as Mum came into the kitchen.

"I beg your pardon!"

He spun around in surprise. "Huh?"

She stood in front of him. She can be quite intimidating when in cop mode. "My sons' friends say *excuse me* and *don't* burp like that. *Especially* without covering their mouths." She gave him what we call the evil eye. Her left brow rose, her eyes narrowed, and her lips pursed. She added a hand on her hip for effect.

Gary withered under that look. "Oh, um, sorry Mrs Gerrome. I, um…" He looked at us and gulped.

We simply stared back.

"I see you didn't leave any for my sons." She stayed in the same spot. "I baked them for all three of you, not just for *you* to inhale." She looked him up and down. "*You*, young man, have *incredibly* rude manners."

He looked ashamedly at the ground. "Um… sorry…"

"Are you?"

He looked up. "What?"

"That's, *pardon*, Mrs Gerrome."

Guilt made him red. "Um, pardon, Mrs Gerrome."

"Are you sorry for your bad, make that, *horrible* lack of manners, and for eating all of the cookies that my sons would have shared with you since you are a *guest in this house*?"

"Um." He panicked and glanced around.

Mike and I were amused. We loved it when Mum ratted someone and was not about to step in.

"Um, yes Mrs Gerrome. Sorry, Mrs Gerrome."

She straightened. "Fine. You can take him downstairs now boys, everything's ready." She gave us a quick look. "I'll be down in a few minutes." She walked off, and after we finished our sodas, we led a very red faced and quiet Gary down to the basement.

"Where are we going?" He stumbled down a few stairs. "Ugh, I don't feel good."

"Would have been all them cookies you swallowed," Mike mumbled in front of him. "It was enough to knock out a horse."

"What knock?" Gary murmured and stumbled off the last step. "What place this?" he managed before face-planting into the middle of the room. Craning his neck, he looked around and managed to roll over. "What place?"

Mike and I stood above him. "It's our basement." I waved a hand around. "We keep our pet snakes down here and a bunch of rats to feed them. We thought you might wanna have a look."

Gary managed to sit up and stared at the wall-to-wall length tanks containing three massive pythons. Red heat lamps glowed upon each snake, and they slithered back and forth in anticipation. On the adjacent wall were rows and rows of small cages filled with rats. All were fattened and ripened for eating. We also had a variety of spiders, lizards and bugs on another wall, but they weren't important right now.

"Has it taken effect?" Mum came down the stairs lugging Gary's bike behind her.

"Bike my why?" Gary asked, using what will he had left to stay in an upright position.

"Oh, it certainly has, hasn't it," she replied after hearing him. "I put enough knockout drug in those cookies for ten boys. Serves you right for stuffing your face." She placed his bike against a bench and pulled out a wire mesh from underneath. "Put this around him and we'll get started. I've locked all the doors, we won't be disturbed."

Mike and I set up the mesh around Gary, who was half sitting, half lying, and clicked the ends together. We stood back and watched as Mum withdrew her book from the locked desk drawer.

"What do you?" Gary swayed. "Happening what?" His eyes rolled back into his head and his body swerved and swung in a circle. "Happening who?"

"We've knocked you out," I told him. "Because you're a bully and need to be taught a lesson."

"Hoolie?" Gary's body stopped.

Mike pointed to the rats and crouched down. "See those rats?"

Gary's eyes focussed. "Hats?"

"They are the boys that have gone missing. All bullies like you, all horrible to others, all deserve what they get. We turn them into rats for our snakes to eat. We turn bullies like you into the rat finks you are. No one will miss you; no one will care…eventually."

"Heat...? Hare...?" mumbled Gary from flat on his back.

"Let's get started," Mum said and turned to a page in her spell book. Mike and I stood on either side of her and we started chanting the spell.

'Blood covered mountains and black driven seas,
White virgin clouds and storm ridden trees,
Take this boy's life and change it for new,
Now turn him to rat, my witch curse upon you.'

We stared down at Gary as his body finally succumbed to the drugs inside. He lay looking up at us, glassy-eyed and tired while we chanted the curse again.

I always wondered what they were thinking at this point. Mum had given us the drug in a very controlled environment. She said we should always understand what happens to people when we drug them and change them. As tenth generation witches, or in our case, wizards, we needed to know repercussions. So I knew what was happening to Gary, but I had no idea what he was thinking.

I watched his right arm twitch...shrink...and change from human arm to rat arm.

"Squeak, squeak, squeak, squeak," was all that came out of Gary's mouth as he saw his arm change. His panicked expression said a whole lot more, but at this stage he was turning and we couldn't understand him. His left hand slapped at his right as his left leg shrank and changed. "Squeak, squeak, squeak." He frantically clawed at it, but stopped when he saw a tail emerge from between his legs. "Squeeeaaakkk."

His right leg and left arm popped in at the same time, and his mouth started changing. His teeth grew long and his nose extended. "Squeeeaakkk." His ears grew up, and he slowly, slowly, shrank...until all that was left of Gary Tackle was a little brown rodent.

We stood staring down at him while he scurried around in circles trying to find a way out of the mesh cage.

Mum closed her book and locked it away. "Well, that's enough fun for today. Take care of him and come upstairs. I made a stew for dinner. We'll take care of his bike later."

She headed upstairs and Mike stepped into the ring of mesh, cornered Gary, and picked him up by the tail. He dangled him in front of his face. "Thought you could bully everyone, didn't you?" He swung him back and forth. "Now you're gonna find out what it's like to be the victim of a snake."

I'd picked up the mesh, but now stood watching as Mike pulled back a glass panel on Hugo's tank. We had named our snakes and Hugo was Mike's. Mine was Teldra and lay on the shelf below, and Mum's was an albino called Festa, who took the crown position on the top shelf.

Mike dangled a struggling Gary into the tank and Hugo came up for air. He'd been watching the whole thing, flicking his tongue, and eyeing off the rodent before him in excited anticipation of his meal. Now, he had dinner handed to him.

Chomp.

One mouthful and Gary was gone.

Mike replaced the glass and stood watching as Hugo slid into the corner and curled up around himself to digest his food.

I put the mesh away and picked a rat for Teldra who was eagerly waiting for his own dinner. Mike chose a fat white rat for Festa, and then we went upstairs to feed ourselves.

Just one more day in the lives of the Gerrome St Johns.

I caught the waft of the stew on the stove and felt my pupils narrow into slits. My forked tongue slithered out to lick my lips, and my stomach growled at the aromas making their way into my nostrils. I always did love Mum's human and rat stew.

HU-BOT, I AM

"Whoa, dude, did you see the new technology those scientists have come up with?" Marcus barged into my bedroom, threw his bag on the floor, and slapped a magazine open on the desk in front of me. "They've found a way to give people new life by making them robotic arms and legs and stuff." He pointed to a picture in the article displaying a group of white-coated doctors standing around a bed with a half drugged outpatient who had a new robo-arm. "They say it's just in the early stages and are practising on people who volunteer. That is *so* cool." He sat on my bed. "Just think, we'll all be the next wave of scientifically engineered walking, talking human robots."

I finished reading the article and studied the photo. It sounded too good to be true, and from the look of the arm in the photo, it *looked* too good to be true. I turned to Marcus. "They have been saying for a while they were looking at doing this. I guess they got themselves a guinea pig in this patient." I studied the man's face. I couldn't read his expression, but I seriously wondered how happy he was going to be with it when he was wide awake and able to use it. *If he was able to use it.* "Other scientists have come out and debunked it all, claiming the doctors are forcing people into having the surgery and then they disappear after, never to be seen again."

I closed the magazine and looked at the cover. A half man half robot hybrid was front and centre, all computer generated, of course, since no one knew if this person even existed. The man's arms and legs were robotics, and he had plates in his head and neck. The magazine's caption read, *'Hu-bots and Ro-mans. The new breed of living beings'.*

"New breed of living beings," I muttered. "Robots can't actually breed, anyway, and it's not like they're actually *alive*, so they're *not living*." I threw the mag at Marcus. "What a load of hogwash."

"It's hardly hogwash; it's the dawn of a new era in robotic engineering." He flicked through the magazine. "If I lost an arm or leg I'd want it replaced with a robotic one. I think it's cool." Glancing up, he added, "Besides, they're not that far advanced from the prosthetic arms and legs we have now."

"The ones we have now aren't robotic and don't want to take over the world one day."

Marcus snorted. "Take over the world! You've been watching way too many movies."

"Yes, and robots take over the world," I protested. "Why would we want that? They'll get in our computer systems and start running everything and then we'd be stuffed as humans. We'd have to go back to the pioneer days and ways and no one wants that." I spun around in my chair. "Can *you* live without your PC and the internet?"

Marcus frowned. "I seriously doubt the robots will be able to take over the world, so we won't have to live without technology, Sam. You're just being ridiculous."

"You didn't answer my question."

Marcus stopped and grimaced.

"Yeah, thought so." I smiled. "You couldn't go without your tech gadgets or the internet. You'd be lost without them."

"Well…" Marcus started and then laughed. "Yeah, you're probably right. Doesn't mean I don't think these robotic limbs aren't cool though."

*****

Over the next few weeks, the article spread like wildfire. Every magazine, TV show, and website wanted a piece of the new robotic arm the scientist had attached to the patient, and Marcus collected and recorded it all. We sat down to watch the *24/7 Weekly News* episode that was all about the arm, the man attached to it, and the scientist who made them both.

"So, tell me, Dr Schubert," Mike Moore, the *24/7* current affairs reporter started from his chair in the warmly lit room in which they sat. "When did you even *think* of using robotics in humans?"

The tall, thin, moustached man sitting in a

straight back chair smiled. "Robotics have been around for a very long time, Mr Moore." His French accent flowed smoothly from between his thin lips. "The idea of robotics in prosthesis is not new. Think back to the claw; it could turn and open and close. Then we came up with the moving hands. All of these stages picked up on nerve endings and thought patterns, essentially, using the body to operate the new hand. So, it was not a very big step to take it to the next level of robotics."

"Like the old '70s TV show, *The Six Million Dollar Man*?" Moore cut in.

"Well…" Schubert smiled grimly and pursed his lips. "We are much more sophisticated than that these days."

"Are these robotic arms controlled by the brain?"

"Absolutely," Schubert replied and picked up the arm lying on the table beside him. "These arms are just a few stages on from the current prosthetics; the only difference is, they have more robotics and have been designed to meld with the host, er, I mean, human." He reddened under the lights, but continued. "The legs will do the same. And we are looking into a circuitry system to attach to other parts, such as the brain, heart, and other vital organs."

"Will they be robotic as well?" Moore stared in fascination at the arm Schubert was turning around.

So were we.

"Yes, in a sense. They will be pumps and electrifiers for people who have irregular heartbeats or mental issues contained by electrical currents. The circuits will be able to send currents to the nerve or organ to keep it beating properly. They'll send the current to the pulse through the part it's attached to, to keep it regular."

"Tell us." Moore pointed his pen at the arm. "Show us how this arm works."

Schubert held it up and slowly turned it over and around.

As much as I hate the thought of robotics taking over the world, it did look incredibly impressive.

He pointed inside the arm. "We fit the stump into this section here." He flicked a couple of switches and the upper arm opened. "You can see it better this way. We fit the stump here, and attach the nerves to the wiring here." The wiring was lit up like a Christmas tree, all pulsating and throbbing on white high beam. It looked a little like a million fibre optics bunched together. "The current is fed through the nerves, and within minutes becomes one with the nervous system of the patient. That will allow them to move it back and forth, move the fingers, and the hand. Everything a normal human arm does, this robotic arm will do just as well. Then we enclose the arm like this." He clicked shut the top flaps he'd opened for a closer look. "The robot arm encloses around the human arm and stays that way unless it needs to be upgraded. By the time this wears out, we will have *even more* sophisticated robotics in place to replace it with." He put the arm back on the table and looked lovingly at it.

He's clearly proud of himself and what he's achieved, I thought.

"Before long, we will be walking, talking human robots, or robotic humans." He ran his fingers over his thin moustache. "It is *very* impressive, no?"

Mike Moore sat back in his seat and let a gush of breath out. "Yes, Dr Schubert, very impressive indeed. So, is that where the names Hu-bot and Ro-man come from?"

Schubert's top lip twitched. "We're not entirely sure where those terms came from. We certainly didn't make them up ourselves, and the magazine that ran the story claim they didn't make them up either."

"But isn't that what these people are, half human, half robot? Hence the terms, Hu-bot and Ro-mans?"

"They are hardly half and half," Schubert snapped. "An arm or a leg does not constitute a half robot. They are simply the prosthesis of the future."

"Will they take over the future?" Moore asked. "They're essentially computers. Will they end up taking over the world?"

"In terms of prosthesis, we hope so." Schubert pursed his lips once more.

"Will they be more than just arms and legs? Will it be one day possible to replace a whole body with a robotic one? Isn't that what Ro-man is? Robot-Human."

Schubert's nervous twitch started again. "I'm sure that will be something to happen in the future, but for now, that is a long way off."

"Considering the Asian countries are making robots to work for them, it can't be too far away to think we will be part robot one day?" Moore waited for the answer, but was clearly agitated that he wasn't getting the answers he wanted.

Schubert uncrossed then re-crossed his legs. "Well, that's something you'll have to talk to them about." His face had remained stony cold and unmoving, except for the twitch and the loving look at his robot arm, during the whole interview. You could see that he was annoyed, angry even, and was wishing the interview was over.

"I think it's time we spoke to the patient, the man you operated on last month. We'll be back in a moment," Moore signed off and the show went to commercial break.

We sat back in our seats. "Whoa," I heard beside me and looked to see Marcus wide-eyed and open-mouthed, staring at the screen.

"What did you think of that doctor?" I asked. "He seems a bit shady to me, like he's hiding something."

"*Did you see that arm?* That would be *so cool* to have." Marcus hadn't moved. "That would be *so* cool."

"What? Being half a robot? No, thanks." I got up and grabbed us a couple of sodas from the fridge and was back just as the show started again.

"Now we talk to the patient, the first person to have a successful robotic arm transplanted on to his own amputated human one."

The show ran the back story on the patient. A thirty-four year old Asian man, a hard worker, lost his arm in an accident, but couldn't afford prosthetics. He was put up for the trial and was chosen, receiving the robotic arm he had today. He was sitting in a physiotherapy room somewhere in China, learning how to use his new arm. The camera zoomed in on the fingers moving, the wrist turning, the man waving hello.

He smiled. Not the happy *on top of the world* smile you'd think he'd have, but a tired, half scared out if his wits, *I don't know what I'm doing or who these people are*, smile. There was a translator sitting beside him.

"He says he is still getting used to having the arm after losing his own." She paused. "But he hopes after getting used to the arm, it will be like he never lost his."

The camera pulled in tight on the man's face, and Moore's voice sounded off screen. "How does the arm feel?"

The man, whose name was Ween Ma Chin, spoke to the translator.

"He says it feels very heavy and makes his body tingle all over. He has been told this is the electrical impulses connected to his nerves."

"When he lost his arm, was it an easy choice to enter that trial on the thin hope he'd be chosen?" The camera zoomed in on the fingers opening and closing into a fist.

Voices mumbled.

"Ah, yes. He was worried because he could not afford a prosthetic, so he could not work, and he was worried he wouldn't be chosen for the robotic arm, but he was, and now he will be able to return to work eventually."

"Does having a robotic arm worry him?"

The camera focussed on Ween Ma Chin's face then panned out so he and the interpreter were in the frame together.

"At the moment, yes. Because I have to get used to using it. But as long as it will allow me to work in the future, I'm sure I will stop worrying."

We saw a few more camera shots of him doing physio such as picking up an empty glass and taking it to his lips. Finally, the screen cut back to Mike Moore, standing in front of a human sized robot.

"Is this the way of the future? Making and attaching robotic arms, legs and plates to the human body to replace lost limbs, or to send electrical impulses to the organs that need regulating? Will humans become robots? Will the robotic parts overtake and override the human within us? Within each limb or plate is a computer chip the size of your little fingernail. It runs the limbs or plate and is almost indestructible. How are we meant to deal with this?" He waved a hand in front of the robot and it made the same hand movement.

"With the electrical system taking over our nervous system, does that mean we will be overcome? That eventually, the computer within the chip will control us? Control our brain, our heart, our feelings, the way we think, what we say and do? And where is that computer connected; a main hub for some bigwig scientific company, the government? Who will control that super computer? Who will be in charge of running it and the robotic prosthesis that people start getting? Will we be overrun as a nation? Controlled as a nation? We all know what happened in *The Terminator* movies, when computers and robots took control. It was the end of life as we knew it." He waved his hand in front of the robot once more and received the same motion in reply. "So, do we really want to partake in such experiments that could very well lead to the destruction of the human race? From Zhing Zhan, China, I'm Mike Moore for *24/7 Weekly News.*"

I sat back on my seat and took a breath; blinked a few times, sculled back the rest of my drink, and finally turned to Marcus. "I told you I wasn't the only one worried they'd take over the world."

His eyes were glazed over and he sat unmoving, still staring at the TV, undrunk soda still in his hand.

I nudged him. "You okay, or are you hypnotised by your favourite subject?" I changed the channel and put something with more life on.

"That…was…awesome! I want a robotic arm!"

I turned my head so fast I pulled a nerve in my neck. "Don't be stupid! They're high tech prosthetics for people who've lost their limbs through accidents or disease. You don't just get one because they look cool or awesome."

Marcus rolled his eyes. "Obviously, Sam, geez. But even just like a fake one, you know. Walking around with it on my arm would be so cool." He twisted his arm back and forth imagining the way it would look.

I sighed. "I still think having a robotic limb or a computer chip attached to your head or heart would be a bad thing. Who knows who would be controlling it and do God knows what to you. They could programme you to rob banks and kill people or even…even…commit suicide." I shook my head. "Nope, no way you'd ever get me picking one of those limbs. I'd rather get a normal prosthetic, or just go without."

"For God's sake, Sam." Marcus stood and got ready to leave. "Would you *really* go without an arm just out of fear of being controlled?"

I stood up too. "I didn't say that. I said, I'd rather a normal prosthetic, *or* just go without. There is still a choice." I walked Marcus to the door.

"Well, either way," he said, walking onto the porch. "You're still nuts. Night."

"Night." I shook my head and locked up. There was no way in hell I'd have one of those computer chip controlled things attached to me. Nope, no way in hell.

*****

A couple of weeks later, Marcus came racing over to my place. He only lived three houses down the street, so it didn't take him long.

"Oh, my God, oh, my God, oh, my God. *Guess*

what they're doing?" He threw himself on my bed and waited until I answered. Which I didn't. "Well, aren't you going to guess?"

"Nope, just tell me." I went back to the report I was typing up for school.

"*They're bringing the robotic limbs here to Australia.* They've been approved for trials, and if it's a success, we'll be doing it for amputees." Marcus bounced up and down. "*This is so cool.*"

I spun my seat so I was facing him. "You're kidding? The government is allowing those robot things into the country?" I shook my head in amazement. "*How could they?* How could they allow that company, those things, to be trialled here? There will be destruction left, right and centre. The company, the government, will control those limbs and the people who have them. It's wrong, and I hope there's a petition to stop it. It will be the end of us as we know it."

Marcus sighed and stopped bouncing. "You really are a party pooper, Sam. Why can't you see it's the way of the future? The prosthetics we have now are about to get better because of these robotic limbs. If it helps people, good. Why are you being such a wet blanket?"

His stare unnerved me and I turned away. "It's not the limbs I have an issue with; it's the whole robot human thing. Who controls the computer chip in them? What if it gets into the wrong hands?" I glanced at him. "It *could* do massive amounts of damage and be very destructive. I do *not want* someone else controlling me through fake limbs—"

"Arrrggghhhh…"

We stopped and pricked our ears.

"My baby…"

We ran for the door and bolted down to the road. Marcus and I lived on a main road and opposite us was a woman screaming for help.

"Help…my baby…"

Frantically glancing around, we saw a toddler wandering on the median strip in the middle of traffic hour.

Without thinking of my own safety, I bolted across the lane, scooped up the baby, and hung on for dear life. The boy screamed and squirmed, and when it was safe, I dashed across the road to hand the wormy squirmy kid back to its mother.

"Oh, my God, thank you, thank you." She hugged and kissed the baby and chastised it at the same time. "You silly little boy, how could you scare Mummy by running off." She glanced my way. "Thank you so much for saving my baby."

"You're welcome, just keep him on a leash." I turned and stepped onto the road straight into the path of an oncoming truck.

I hadn't meant to.

Step in front of a truck, I mean.

I stupidly didn't look for the traffic and stupidly stepped out onto the road.

The driver hit the brakes with a loud squeal and smoking tyres, but it was too late. He was too fast and too close, and I was too small and too stupid.

He hit me full force with his head high massive truck bull bars, and with a sickening thud and crunch, I went flying through the air like a lifeless rag doll. The truck skidded after me and stopped barely a half metre from where I landed in a crumpled broken mess.

I lay staring at the tyres, just within reach, so close I could touch them if I tried. But I couldn't. I couldn't move. I couldn't breathe. I could barely hear and see. It was all blurry with pain. A hot searing, burning pain all through my body.

I think I'm dead.

Not that I know what dead feels like.

The truck driver was frantically walking around me, directing traffic to stop and talking into a phone.

I saw a blurry Marcus race over to me and crouch down beside, calling my name. "Sam… Sam…"

It was as if I was underwater. The sounds were all buried under the noise in my ears. I felt the gravel and tar beneath me. Smelt the aroma of them in my nostrils. I was lying on my right side, the side hit by the truck. Somehow, I'd gone flying sideways through the air, only to have my legs fly past me, underneath me, so I landed on the side I was hit.

Shouldn't I have gone flying head first into something?

I don't know. I do know I'm hot and wet and people are moving around me. Is that sirens? Yes, louder now, and now I see cops in their uniforms crowding around and pushing other people back.

I'm tired. So tired. And hot and wet and thirsty. I

want a drink. Mmm…a nice cold Pepsi Max would go down so good right now. More sirens, more people in uniforms. Ambulances. Or is that Ambuli? What's the plural of ambulance? I don't know, so tired…

"Sam…Sam…can you hear me?"

Someone flashed a light in my eyes and poked and prodded me.

Something hard is being wrapped around my neck. I think it's a brace. They must think my neck's broken. Maybe they're right, coz I can't feel anything below my waist, and I can see one leg sticking out in front of me. Wait, I'm being strapped onto something hard.

Uniformed men crowded around me and rolled me onto my back.

I sigh and feel more pain.

My ribs are killing me, my right shoulder feels crushed. My body feels like it has imploded.

The sky is so blue…

My eyes move in every direction, taking in as much as possible. I'm surprised I'm hanging on. *Clearly I'm not dying, unless it's a slow death. And a painful one at that.*

I'm pushed into the ambulance and the cops shut the doors.

"Sam…" the ambo said. "We're getting you to hospital; hang on." He fiddled with knobs and tubes as we raced for the nearest hospital.

I still couldn't move or talk or feel anything below my waist.

I hope I haven't peed myself, now that would be so embarrassing.

I had no concept of time, or much else, but we came to a halt, the doors were ripped open, and I was wheeled into the city's biggest hospital.

"Sam, Sam, oh my poor baby."

Mum?

She ran to me and leant over, doing what I thought was pushing my hair off my face. "You'll be okay, Sammy, I love you."

I was wheeled into a room and curtains were drawn all around. Nurses, doctors, what seemed like hundreds of them, all crowded around me, poking, prodding, sticking me with things. They moved a machine over me and left the room. The machine moved up and down my body, stopping periodically before moving on.

What is that? X-ray?

I heard mumbling somewhere in the distance and everyone swarmed back in, crowding around again, sticking more tubes and needles in. *My head is screaming, ugh, the pain.* It sounded like an incredibly loud whistle in my ear. I managed to move my eyeballs downwards to see a doctor talking to my parents at the end of the bed.

His hands moved quickly in time with his words, not that I could hear his words, but I saw his mouth move; a mouth with thin lips and a thin moustache above them.

Why does he look familiar?

Tall and thin with slicked back hair, he finally looked at me and I knew who he was.

Dr Schubert!

My head raced and I wanted to scream at him to go away.

"His heart is speeding up, we need to get him under, stat." The French accent was loud and clear as he came to my side and flicked his light into my eyes.

Don't you bloody dare, Frenchie! I tried to say, but couldn't so I hoped I conveyed the message with the expression in my eyes.

He looked surprised, as though he had read that expression, but then smiled that slick little Frenchman smile of his and nodded. "Yes, he'll make a very good candidate indeed."

*****

I don't remember much after that. Everything went black. For how long, I have no idea, but I vaguely remember waking a few times en route to somewhere. At one stage it felt as though I was flying, but the doctor quickly put an end to me being awake. Another time, I was in hospital. I don't think it was the one from home. It looked different. It looked cold. It looked foreign. So did the doctors and nurses.

Schubert came to see me. "Hello, Sam. We are going to put you under now. You need surgery to fix your broken bones. It will be a long surgery, but when you wake up, you will be a brand new person."

The hell I will, keep away from me you crazy… person… My eyelids fluttered and closed for the last time.

*****

I have no idea how long I was out, or what country I was in, or even what day it was. But I felt good. Weird, but good. The pain was minimal, and my vision had cleared. The whistling in my ears had subsided, and surprisingly, I was hungry.

I moved my right arm and smashed my hand into my face. "What the hell?" I blinked and stared; I blinked again and kept on staring.

The hand in front of me was not mine.

It was robotic.

"No," I yelled. "No." I checked my left hand. It was still normal. And human. I held my hands side by side out in front of me. One human, one robotic. I followed my right hand up to my shoulder. More robotics. I flung back the covers and saw the rest of me.

"Arrrgghhhh...I'm a robot, arrrgghhhh..."

Almost the whole right side of my body consisted of metal plated robotics, including a whole right arm and leg. There was a plate around my right hip with bolts, and a band that wrapped around my human left hip. There were bolts and wires coming out of each rib, connected to plates that wrapped around my rib cage and chest like a claw. My shoulder was gone and replaced with metal or titanium or whatever the hell they used. I felt my head.

"Arrrgghhhh." My hair was gone and there was a partial helmet attached to my skull on the right side, but still, I was now a half robot. I tried to get out of bed. I wanted to see, I needed a mirror to see.

Thud, thud, thud, thud.

I looked at the door and wondered what was making that noise. A robot thudded into the room. And not just a normal robot…but a robot with a human face.

What the hell!

"I am Ro-man. I have come to see how you are and if you need anything."

I looked it up and down. Shiny silver and black metal, all robot-like. But the face was eerie. It *looked* human…but…weird. Fake, maybe? "What are you? Where am I? *What* am I?" I surprised myself by talking as I wasn't sure if I could. I felt a tingle down my spine and pushed myself up onto my new robo-arm. "Argh." I grimaced at the pain still not yet healed, and extended my human arm behind me, feeling my spine covered in bolts and nodes and wires.

"*What the hell happened to me?*" I screamed. "*I didn't want this. I didn't want this.*" I collapsed onto the bed and the robot picked up the covers and pulled them over me.

"Your parents gave Dr Schubert permission. Your body was crushed by the accident and they could not save it. It needed replacing." It stood beside the bed looking down at me. An eerie human face in a metal body. Silicon? Real skin? Ugh! "You needed to be replaced."

"I *never* wanted this. I *never* wanted a robotic anything. Get rid of it, take it away. Give me normal prosthetics." I burst into tears. *"I didn't want this. I want my parents. I want to go home."*

"You cannot go home until you are better, and it will take a long time for you to get better. It will be a big adjustment." It stared down with glassy-looking human eyes.

"What the hell are you?" I sobbed. "You're a freak show." I glanced down at myself. "And now I am too."

"I am Ro-man. You are now Hu-bot. We are different, not the same."

Its voice was like a computer generated human voice. Kind of like Siri in Apple's iPhones.

"I am not a Hu-bot," I screamed. *"Never!"*

"I am Ro-man. You are Hu-bot," it repeated. "I am Ro-man. Robot with human brain and face. You are Hu-bot. Human with robotic parts. We are different, not the same."

"I am not a Hu-bot," I screamed again as nurses and orderlies came rushing in. *"I am not a Hu-bot. Where are my parents? I want to go home."* I thrashed in my bed trying to move, trying to get up. Trying to fight. *"I am not a Hu-bot,"* I repeated at the top of my voice as I was stabbed with something sharp from the inside.

I gasped and stopped crying. "What was that?" I felt warmth surge after the pain.

"I adjusted the computer to calm your nerves. It works from the inside and doesn't waste injections."

"Stop it," I yelled, knowing it was exactly as I had feared. I felt myself falling. "I want to go home.

I want my parents. I want...to be...human...I am not...a Hu-bot...I am not a...” I felt myself falling into darkness. “...Hu-bot...I...am...”

ABOUT THE AUTHOR

T.K. is a children's TV show veteran who loves watching disaster and creature/zombie movies and TV shows, but not at night.

T.K. started writing many a year ago back in primary school, but only started her author career in 2015 with the release of her first three stories and anthology. She will write and release stories until there are twelve *Bones* books and a special edition numbered 13...

T.K. lives in Australia, loves extra cheesy cheeseburgers and chocolate, and gets a kick out of watching funny dog and cat videos.

T.K. Wrathbone is the kid's/tween pen name for author Tiara King. You can find more about Tiara on her website; follow her on social media, or visit her publishing house, Royal Star Publishing.

SOCIALS

tkwrathbone.com

tiaraking.com.au

royalstarpublishing.com.au

Sign up for *Tiara's* Newsletter…

Make sure you're always in the know and never miss free exclusives, the latest news, book updates, and so much more with newsletters from…

tiaraking.com.au

HAVE YOU READ THESE?

Next Top Mannequin
Cinderfella and Princess Charming: Witch Hunters
www.badluck-youredead.com
The Bones of Wrath: Changes
One Bone: Anthology 1

The Orphanage
Hantel and Gresel: Food Critics
Mirror, Mirror On The Wall
The Bones of Wrath: Haunted
Two Bone: Anthology 2

The Howler
Shadow Walkers
Faded
The Bones of Wrath: Ghosts
Three Bone: Anthology 3

I Spy With My Little Eye
Knock, Knock…Who's Dead?
It Creeped At Midnight
The Bones of Wrath: Monsters
Four: Anthology 4

OR THESE?

Trick Or Treat
All Hallows Possession
They Rise On A Blood Moon
The Bones of Wrath: Horrors
Five Bone: Anthology 5

All Clowns Must Die!
The Demon Resides
Infestation
The Bones of Wrath: Terrors
Six Bone: Anthology 6

www.ingramcontent.com/pod-product-compliance
Lightning Source LLC
Chambersburg PA
CBHW032105180726
48284CB00002B/460